$3.75

The Glass Bees

by ERNST JUENGER

Translated from the German by
Louise Bogan *and* Elizabeth Mayer

The marionettes turned out at the Zapparoni works are handsomer than human beings. Their performance is so lifelike, one cannot believe that they are machines. But they are not the only automata made at the plant and though Zapparoni conceives of himself as a benefactor of mankind, he requires the help of adventurers who have a stomach for anything. The hero of this novel, Captain Richard, is such a man and this extraordinary book tells the story of an afternoon spent in the garden adjoining the factory. Hard-up, *persona non grata* almost everywhere, Richard, former cavalry officer and professional soldier, is desperately in need of work; yet, what he finds at the Zapparoni plant is too much for even him. Zapparoni's world is the world of the glass bees and antithetical to all that is natural and human. Not since Huxley's *Brave New World* has there been a book

(*continued on back flap*)

T H E   G L A S S   B E E S

by Ernst Juenger

Translated from the German by
LOUISE BOGAN *and* ELIZABETH MAYER

The Noonday Press
a subsidiary of
Farrar, Straus and Cudahy

Grateful acknowledgment is made to the resourceful and acute editorial help of Ruth Limmer, in the final stages of this translation.

Louise Bogan

I

When we were hard up, Twinnings had to step in. This time I had waited too long: I should have decided to see him sooner, but misery undermines the will. As long as one still has some small coins to jingle together, one hangs around the cafés, staring into empty space. My run of bad luck seemed endless. I still had one suit in which I looked reasonably presentable, unless I crossed my legs. There were holes in my shoes. In such a situation solitude is preferable.

I had served with Twinnings in the Light Cavalry, and he frequently had given me and other comrades advice. He had good connections. After listening to me, he pointed out that I could count only on jobs with a catch to them. I knew this was the truth; I could not afford to be fastidious.

We were friends, which did not mean much, since Twinnings was friendly with nearly everyone he knew, except those with whom he was on bad terms at the moment. That was his business. He spoke to me without reservation, which did not embarrass me because it was rather like consulting a doctor who makes a thorough examination and does not waste words. He felt the lapel of my coat, testing the material. Suddenly I saw the spots on it, as if my vision had been sharpened.

He then discussed my situation in detail. A good part of me was, as it were, consumed, and though I had experienced much, I had accomplished little that might serve as reference. I had to admit that. The best jobs, those coveted by everyone, brought in a large income without involving too much work. But I did not have relatives who could bestow honors and commissions, like Paul Domann, for example, whose father-in-law built locomotives and earned more money at breakfast than people who, year in year out, slaved on Sundays and weekdays. The larger the objects you peddle, the easier it is; a locomotive can be sold quicker than a vacuum cleaner.

But I did have an uncle—a former senator, long since dead —nobody remembers him now. My father had lived the quiet life of a civil servant; the little he left me had long since disappeared, and I had married a poor girl. I could not make a great show of a dead senator or of a wife who comes to the door herself when the doorbell rings.

Jobs existed which involved much work and decidedly little pay. You sold refrigerators and washing machines from house to house until you were almost seized with doorbell panic. If you visited old war-comrades, they were, of course, resentful when you attacked them, all unsuspecting, with a life insurance policy. Smiling, Twinnings avoided saying anything about this sort of job, and I was grateful. He could, with reason, have asked me if I hadn't learned anything better.

He knew, of course, that I had once been employed in testing tanks, but he also knew that I was on the black list. Later I shall come back to this episode.

The rest were jobs with a risk attached. They provided a comfortable life, sufficient means, but troubled sleep. Twinnings mentioned a few of these—they resembled police jobs. Who nowadays did not have his own police? Times were unsafe. Life and property had to be protected, real estate and transportation closely guarded, blackmail and crime counteracted. Presumption increased in proportion to philanthropy. Anyone who reached a certain prominence could no longer rely on public protection; he had to have a cudgel in the house.

But even in this special field supply was greater than demand. All the good jobs were already filled. Twinnings had a great many friends and times were not propitious for ex-soldiers. There was, for instance, Lady Boston, an immensely rich and still youthful widow, who continually trembled for her children's safety, particularly since capital punishment for kidnapping had been abolished. But Twinnings had already attended to this.

Another case was that of Preston, the oil magnate, who was obsessed with horses. Like an ancient Byzantine, he was crazy about his stables—a hippomaniac, who did not spare any expense to satisfy his passion. His horses were treated like demigods. Everyone tries to distinguish himself in some way and Preston considered horses more satisfying to his ambition than fleets of oil tanks and forests of derricks. His horses also drew royalty to his house. At the same time this passion brought with it a lot of trouble. Everyone had to be closely watched in the stables, and during transport as well as on the race track. Conspiracies among the jockeys, jealousies of other horse-fanciers, passions linked with high betting, were constant menaces. No *diva* has to be so carefully guarded as a race horse entered for the *grand prix*. This is a job for an old cavalryman, a man with a good eye and a heart for horses. But Tommy Gilbert already had the job and had found work for half of his cavalry unit too. He was the apple of Preston's eye.

Twinnings ticked off these jobs one after another, as a chef would name the most delicious items no longer on a menu. This is a trait peculiar to all agents. He wished to whet my appetite. Finally he arrived at tangible offers; now you could be sure that there was more than one fly in the ointment.

The person in question was Giacomo Zapparoni, one of those men who have money to burn—although his father had crossed the Alps, penniless and on foot. You couldn't open a newspaper or a magazine or sit in front of a movie screen without coming upon his name. His plant was quite near, and by exploiting both his own and foreign inventions, he had achieved a monopoly in his field.

Journalists wrote fantastic stories about the objects he manufactured. "To those who have, shall be given." Probably their imagination ran wild. The Zapparoni Works manufactured robots for every imaginable purpose. They were supplied on special order, and in standard models which could be found in every household. It was not a question of big automatic machines as one might think at first. Zapparoni's speciality was lilliputian robots. With a few exceptions their scale increased to the size of a watermelon and decreased to something the size of a Chinese curio. On the smaller scale they gave the impression of intelligent ants, distinct units working as mechanisms, that is, not at all in a purely chemical or organic fashion. This was one of Zapparoni's business principles or, if you will, one of the rules of his game. When faced with two solutions, it seemed as if he almost always preferred the more subtle one. This choice corresponded with the trend of the times, and he was not the worse for it.

Zapparoni had started with tiny turtles—he called them "selectors"—which were designed for picking and choosing.

They could count, weigh, sort gems or paper money and, while doing so, eliminate counterfeits. The principle involved was soon extended; they worked in dangerous locations, handling explosives, dangerous viruses, and even radioactive materials. Swarms of selectors could not only detect the faintest smell of smoke but could also extinguish a fire at an early stage; others repaired defective wiring, and still others fed upon filth and became indispensable in all jobs where cleanliness was essential. My uncle, the senator, who all his life suffered from hay fever, no longer had to retreat to the mountains after Zapparoni had put selectors, trained for pollen, on the market.

His apparatuses soon became irreplaceable, not only to industry and science but also to the housewife. They saved labor and introduced a human atmosphere, unknown until now, into the factory. A resourceful mind had discovered a gap which no one had seen, and had filled it. This is the best way to do business, the best way to make a fortune.

Yet in Zapparoni's case the shoe pinched. Twinnings, for one, did not know the exact details, but one could roughly guess. Now and then he had difficulties with his workers. If someone is ambitious enough to force dead matter to think, he cannot do without original minds. Moreover, the measurements in question were infinitesimal. In the beginning, probably, it was less difficult to create a whale than a hummingbird.

Zapparoni had a staff of highly skilled experts. He greatly preferred that the inventors, who brought him their models, take on permanent employment with him, where they either reproduced their inventions or modified them. This was chiefly necessary in those departments where the objects, toys for instance, were dependent on fashion. Before the era of Zapparoni, no one had ever seen such fantastic toys—he created a lilliputian realm, a pygmy world, which made not only children but grown-ups forget time in a dreamlike trance. The toys went far beyond human imagination. But every year, for Christmas, this lilliput theater had to be re-decorated with new settings and a new cast of characters.

The wages of Zapparoni's employees equaled those of professors or even government officials. He was amply repaid. Should any of his workers give notice, it would mean irreparable loss, if not catastrophe for him, particularly if they chose to work elsewhere, either in this country or, still worse, abroad. Zapparoni's wealth and monopoly rested not only upon his firm's secret but upon a special technique, which could be acquired only in the course of decades and then not by everyone. And this technique was dependent on the workers, upon their hands, upon their brains.

To be sure, they had little inclination to quit a place where they were so well-treated and so royally paid. There were, however, exceptional cases. It's an old truth that man cannot always be satisfied. Apart from that, the people employed by Zapparoni were an extremely difficult lot. Engaged in a most peculiar kind of work—the handling of minute and often extremely intricate objects—they gradually developed an eccentric, over-scrupulous behavior, and they developed personalities which took offence at the motes in a sunbeam. They could find flaws in everything. They were artists who had to measure objects of the size of a flea, provide them with horseshoes, and screw them on. This was very close to pure fantasy. Zapparoni's world of automatons, sufficiently uncanny in itself, was the setting for minds which indulged in the strangest whims. It was rumored that scenes frequently took place in his private office similar to those which occur in the office of the chief physician of a lunatic asylum. Unfortunately, robots capable of manufacturing robots do not yet exist. That would be the philosophers' stone, the squaring of the circle.

Zapparoni had to face the facts. His geniuses were part of the character of his factory, and he handled them with diplomatic skill. He left the models to them while he reserved for himself the manipulation of men, displaying all the charm and flexibility of an Italian impresario. In doing so, he reached the limit of the possible. To be exploited by Zapparoni was the dream of every young man with a technical bent. Zapparoni hardly ever lost his self-control or his affability, but when he did, terrifying scenes followed.

Naturally, he tried to protect himself in the employment contracts, though in a most agreeable manner. The contracts were drawn up for a lifetime, with provisions for gradual wage increases, for premiums, insurance, and, in the case of breach of contract, penalties. The employee who had signed a contract with Zapparoni and could call himself "master" or "author" was a man whose success was assured. He had his own house, his own car, and his paid vacation on Teneriffe or in Norway.

There were some restrictions, it is true—scarcely noticeable however—that actually added up to a well-devised control system. Various arrangements served this purpose: they were marked with the innocent labels which today disguise a secret service—one of them was called, I believe, the Clearing House. The lists kept on every single employee in the Zapparoni Works resembled police dossiers. Only they went into more detail. Nowadays a person has to be *mentally* X-rayed in order to find out what to expect from him, because the temptations are enormous.

All this was perfectly correct. To take precautions against breaches of confidence is one of the duties of the manager of a great industry. To assist Zapparoni in protecting the secrets of his firm proved that one was on the side of the law.

What happened, then, if one of the experts gave notice, or simply left and paid the penalty? Here was a weak point in Zapparoni's system. After all, he could not detain anyone by force; it was a great risk. It was in his own interest, therefore, to demonstrate that either form of absconding would prove undesirable. There are, we know, many ways and means to turn the screws on a person, particularly when money doesn't count.

In the first place, you can saddle him with lawsuits. They have already taught many a man a lesson. The law, however, was not without gaps; for some time now it lagged behind technical development. What, for example, could the right of "authorship" be called in such a case? Wasn't it the glory, which the head of a team radiated, rather than personal merit, a glory that could not simply be detached and taken along? And wasn't it the same with artistic skill, developed in the course of thirty or forty years with the help and at the expense of the plant? This skill was not the property of a single individual. The individual was indivisible—or wasn't he? These were problems which the primitive mind of a policeman could hardly solve. Confidential positions presuppose independent thinking. The essential has to be guessed at; it was not mentioned, either in writing or by word of mouth. It must be grasped intuitively.

All this I roughly gathered from Twinnings' remarks, which were a mixture of logic and guesswork. Perhaps he knew more, perhaps less. In such cases the less said, the better. I already understood enough; Zapparoni was looking for a man to do the dirty work.

The job was not for me. I shall not speak of morality—that would be ridiculous. I had served through the whole Asturian civil war. In that kind of warfare no one's hands stay clean, high or low, right or left. You met types with a list of sins which would have staggered case-hardened father confessors. Of course, they would not have dreamed of going to confession; on the contrary, when they got together they were high-spirited, even boastful, as the Bible says, of their misdeeds. People with tender consciences were not popular with them. But they had their own moral code. Not one of them would have accepted the job that Twinnings proposed to me

—not so long as he wished to keep the respect of the others, whatever the color of his skin. He would have been excluded from their comradeship, from their drinking bouts, from their camp. His comrades would not have trusted him, would have been tongue-tied in his presence, and would not expect his aid in an emergency. Even prisoners and galley slaves are extremely sensitive on this point.

Therefore, after listening to the story of Zapparoni and his querulous workers, I would have left at once, if Teresa had not been sitting at home, waiting for me. Twinnings was my last straw, and she had set all her hopes upon our meeting.

I am not suited to deal with money or to earn it. Probably Mercury's aspect is unfavorable. This fact becomes more conspicuous as I get older. In our first years together Teresa and I had lived on my demobilization checks, and later we had sold some of our belongings; now there was nothing left to sell. In every household there is a corner where once the lares and penates were assembled, and where today the unsalable objects are kept. In our case these objects were a few racing trophies and other engraved silver left me by my father. Teresa believed I had been sorry to give them up. Her chief worry was that she might be a burden to me; it was her *idée fixe*. But it was I who should have done something long ago—our misery was entirely the result of my own inertia. The sole reason was that I loathed anything connected with business.

I cannot bear the role of a martyr. It makes me furious to be taken for a good man. But Teresa had just this habit: she moved around me as if I were a saint. She saw me in an entirely false light. She should have scolded me, raged, broken vases—but unfortunately she was not that kind of person.

Even as a schoolboy I disliked work. If I was in trouble up to my neck, I wriggled out by developing a temperature. I knew a way to do it. Then I was sent to bed and nursed by my mother with juices and compresses. My cheating didn't worry me at all—I even enjoyed it, but I felt guilty at being pampered like a poor sick child. So in return, I tried to behave intolerably; but the more effectively I acted up, the more everyone worried about my health.

It was almost the same with Teresa; I could not bear to think of her face should I come home without any prospects. When she opened the door, she would instantly read everything in my face.

Possibly I was regarding the whole matter too unfavorably. I was still one mass of useless and antiquated prejudices. Since everything was now supposed to be based on a contract— which was founded neither upon oath nor atonement nor Man—trust and faith no longer existed. Discipline had vanished from the world. It had been replaced by the catastrophe. We were living in permanent unrest, and no one could trust anyone else. Was it *my* responsibility?

Twinnings, watching me sit there, unable to make up my mind, seemed to know my weak point; he said:

"Teresa would most certainly be pleased if you came home with something definite."

I I

This reminded me of the time—long ago—when we had been cadets. Twinnings sat next to me. Even then there was a touch of the middleman about him, and he was on good terms with everybody. It had been a tough time; we weren't treated with kid gloves. Our instructor was Monteron; his presence always cowed us.

Monday was the worst. It was the day of reckoning, the day of judgment. At six in the morning we rode in the *manège*, our heads heavy with sleep. I remember often wishing to be thrown by the horse and taken to the infirmary, but so long as no bones were broken this was out of the question. A "slight temperature"—as at home—did not exist here. Monteron thought these falls very healthy. They were good training and taught you to keep a firm seat.

Our next class was strategy at the sandbox, but the lesson rarely materialized. Monteron, who held the rank of a major, usually entered the classroom scowling like a threatening archangel. Today, naturally, there are still people one is afraid of; but his kind of authority no longer exists. Today one is simply afraid; in those days one had, in addition, a guilty conscience.

The Military Academy was not far from the capital, and the cadet whose pass had not just been canceled, or who was not in the guardhouse, spent his leave there, going by local train, by the horse-drawn streetcar, or in a carriage. Others went on horseback and stabled their horses with relatives: there were still countless stables in town. We would all be in fine fettle, with money in our pockets, since there was no occasion to spend it on the drill grounds. No happier moment existed than the moment when the gates were opened.

On Monday morning everything had a different look. When Monteron entered his office, a pile of unpleasant letters, notices, and reports waited for him on his desk. In addition, there was the sentry's never-failing report that two or three cadets had overstayed their leave and that a fourth hadn't returned at all. Trifles were also reported—the name of a cadet had been taken down because he had smoked in front of the sentry of the Royal Castle, and of another because he had

saluted the commanding officer of the city in a careless way.
More often than not, however, something truly striking occurred. Two cadets had kicked up a row in a bar and had demolished the furniture; another had resisted arrest by drawing
his sabre. These cadets were still locked up somewhere in
town and had to be sent for. Two brothers, on leave of absence for a funeral, had gambled away all their money in
Homburg.

At roll call every Saturday Monteron reinspected our uniforms. After having assured himself that nobody had appeared in "fancy" uniform, by which he meant the slightest
deviation from the regulation, he dismissed us with a few
parting words. He warned us against temptations. And each
time, we rushed off in all directions, convinced of our immu-
nity.

But the city was bewitched—a labyrinth. It laid its snares
cunningly. Each day of furlough was divided into two halves,
one light, the other dark, supper being the fairly exact demar-
cation line. It recalled certain children's books, where on one
page the good, on the other the bad boy is depicted, the only
difference being that in our case the two boys were combined in one person. During the afternoons we visited relatives, sunned ourselves at sidewalk cafés, or strolled in the
Tiergarten. Some of us could even be seen at concerts or
lectures. We presented the ideal picture—Monteron's picture
—youthful, well-behaved, and as neat as a new pin. It was
simply delightful.

In the evenings we had our dates. Either we spent them
alone with our girls or we joined the others. Drinking started
and the atmosphere became, shall we say, more animated.
Later we separated, but at midnight we all met again at Bols
or the English Buffet. As the evening wore on, the places we
visited were more and more doubtful or even explicitly forbidden. At the Viennese Café, frequented by *demimondaines*,
it was easy to clash with the insolent waiters. In the big beer-

halls we had encounters with students, who were keen on picking quarrels. Eventually only a few places were still open, the Everburning Light, for example, and the waiting rooms of the railway stations. Here, most of the people were drunk; in the ensuing brawls there was no glory in winning. At Headquarters these places were notorious, and it was no accident that the military police would arrive at the exact moment when we were involved in a riot. When the spikes of their helmets were seen above the melée, the signal was given: *Sauve-qui-peut.* Often it was too late. They took you along, the patrol leader happy to have nabbed another cadet.

On Monday morning Monteron found the reports on his desk. They arrived by the early train or were telephoned in. Monteron was one of those superior officers who have an especially bad temper in the morning. The blood rushed easily to his head. Then he had to unbutton the collar of his uniform. A bad omen. He could be heard muttering:

"It's incredible where these fellows knock about."

It seemed incredible to us too. There is no difference greater than the one between a thick, aching head in the morning and the identical exuberant head of the night before. Yet it is the very same head. But that we should have been here or there, should have said—or even done—this or that, seemed to us like a story about some third person. It could not and should not be so at all.

Nevertheless, while being chased over the jumps by our riding instructor, we had dark misgivings that something was wrong. When you jump the hurdles with knotted snaffle, elbows tightly propped on your hips, you must have your wits about you. In spite of everything, we sometimes galloped as if in a dream, our minds preoccupied with the events of the night before, which now seemed a bewildering puzzle.

The solution was provided by Monteron at the sandbox, but in a way that exceeded all our fears. Occurrences, which we remembered only dimly and in fragments, now appeared

in a blinding light as an extremely unpleasant whole. Twinnings, who in those days already showed a nimble wit, once de-
clared that it was really unfair to allow sober patrols to hunt
for tipsy youngsters on furlough—the police should be given
a handicap.

Be that as it may—there was hardly a week that did not begin with a terrible dressing-down. Monteron could still open
all the floodgates of authority; this too is a long-lost art. He
was still capable of evoking in us a genuine acceptance of our
misconduct. We had not simply perpetrated this or that. We
had struck at the root of the State; we had endangered the
monarchy. Actually there was a grain of truth in what he
said—though the whole world did what it pleased, without
exciting much notice, freedom being large and general—if a
cadet deviated only slightly, that same world, that same public
opinion, swooped down on him unanimously. This prefigured
the enormous changes which took place soon afterwards.
Monteron probably foresaw them; we cadets were simply
thoughtless.

Looking back, it seems to me that these dressing-downs
turned out, for the most part, far milder than we had expected. We lived in the fear of the Lord. When after the riding
lesson, we changed hurriedly while the room senior goaded us
on—"You are in for something; the Old Man has already
loosened his collar"—it was worse than later when the order
came: "Stand at attention."

Fundamentally, the Old Man had a heart of gold. And in
our hearts we knew it; this explained our intense respect for
him. When he said: "I'd rather keep a bagful of fleas in order
than a class of cadets," he was right, for it wasn't an easy
job. There are superiors who gloat over someone who gets
himself into a hopeless spot since then they can show their
power. Monteron was deeply grieved. And since we knew
this, a cadet who was in a complete fix could go to him in the
evening and confess. When Gronau had gambled all his

money away, Monteron drove to the city that same evening to take care of the matter; although when he returned the next afternoon, it was already too late.

Well, he wanted to harden us, but without injuring our inner core. On Monday mornings orders used to drum upon us like hail—arrest, cancellation of furlough, stable duty, line-up in fatigue dress. But by noon the storm had passed, and we tried, of course, to do our utmost on the drill ground.

In our class two or three cases came up where things took a different turn. Something happened that arrest couldn't remedy. Yet it was remarkable how many things the Old Man could repair by putting us under arrest. In the cases I'm now thinking of, the storm never broke. On the contrary, an oppressed atmosphere prevailed, as if something had happened that should not be referred to or that was only a rumor. There was a coming and going; something went on behind locked doors and afterward the culprit disappeared. His name was never mentioned again, or if it was mentioned, it seemed to happen by mistake, and everyone pretended not to have heard it.

On such days the Old Man, usually relentlessly alert, could be absent-minded, absorbed in his own thoughts. In the classroom he would stop mid-sentence and stare at the wall. Then fragments of a soliloquy might be heard involuntarily rising to his lips; for example: "I could swear that at the bottom of any dishonorable action there is always a woman."

All this rose to the surface of my memory while Twinnings waited for my answer. It had, of course, only a remote relation to the present situation, since Monteron, muttering that sentence, would certainly never have thought of a woman like Teresa. It is nevertheless true that a man will do things for a woman which he would never do for himself.

Such a thing was the job Zapparoni had to offer. I could not say why, yet there are some premonitions which rarely deceive you. No doubt there is a difference between protecting secrets of the State and those of an individual—even in our times, when most States have gone to the dogs. A position like the one offered by Zapparoni would sooner or later lead to an automobile accident. Anyone inspecting the wreckage would find twenty or thirty bullet holes in the back of the car; no case here for the highway patrol. And about the funeral there would be less in the obituaries than on the front page. Teresa would not meet the best people at the open grave, and certainly no one from our better days—not even Zapparoni—would be present. At nightfall, a stranger would deliver an envelope to her.

When my father was buried, things were quite different. He had led a quiet life, but at the end he hadn't been too happy either. Lying sick in bed, he said to me: "My boy, I am dying at just the right moment." Saying this, he gave me a sad, worried look. He had certainly foreseen many things.

These and other matters came into my mind while Twinnings waited for my answer. It is incredible what an avalanche of thoughts can unroll in such a moment. Like a painter, one should be able to compose it all into a picture.

But my mind's eye saw our sparsely furnished apartment, our cold hearth—if I may use this poetic expression to paraphrase the fact that for days now the electricity had been cut off. In the mail were only reminders, and when the doorbell rang, Teresa did not dare answer it, afraid of insolent bill collectors. I had small reason to be fastidious.

On top of everything, I felt ridiculous—I sensed that I was being old-fashioned, one of those people who still wasted their time with scruples, while all the others, who pocketed whatever profit was offered, looked down on me. Together with a great number of others I had twice paid the piper for inefficient governments. We had carried off neither pay nor glory—just the opposite.

It was high time that I discarded my fossil judgments. Only the other day someone had called my attention to the fact that my conversation teemed with superannuated expressions like "old comrades" and "swear on one's sword-knot." These phrases sound funny nowadays, like the affectation of an old spinster who still prides herself on her stale virtue. Hang it all, I had to stop that.

My stomach felt unpleasantly empty. It was, quite simply, hunger; my mouth had a bitter taste. At the same time I felt a slight sympathy for Zapparoni rise in my heart. After all, here at last was someone who showed interest in me. Apart from the great difference in our financial status, he was probably in much the same situation as I was: he too had to pay the price and, to boot, was judged by moral standards. He was fleeced, robbed; and yet he was the exploiter. The government, unhesitatingly obliging to the majority, pocketed his taxes, and allowed him to be bled.

In any case, if "old comrades" sounded funny, why should words like "government" still be taken seriously? Did those figureheads have a monopoly, perhaps, on being serious? Were they an exception to the devaluation of words? Was there, in fact, a person still alive who could teach others the meaning of decency? Even a veteran was no longer respected; but this had its advantages too. The time had come for thinking of one's self—for once.

You see, I had already begun to justify myself—this is the first step when one intends to venture upon something crooked. Strangely enough, no one can simply go ahead and do another person harm. You first have to convince yourself that the other has deserved it. Even a holdup man, about to rob a stranger, will first start a quarrel with him in order to work himself up to real anger.

This was easy for me, since my feelings had reached such a boiling point that almost anyone—no matter how innocent —would be a suitable target for my anger. Even Teresa had once been my victim.

Although I had by now almost decided to accept the offer,

I made one last attempt to back out. I said to Twinnings: "I can't imagine that Zapparoni has been waiting just for me. He must find it rather hard to choose."

Twinnings nodded: "Most of the candidates are people," he said with a gesture, "with a long list of convictions." And he repeated the gesture like a fisherman catching a pike in still waters. Again he had touched a sore spot. Finally my temper gave out.

"Who doesn't have a record, today? Perhaps you, because you've been a smart guy all your life. But otherwise there are only those who were shirkers in war and in peace."

Twinnings laughed. "Don't get excited, Richard—we all know you don't have a flawless record. But in your case there's a difference: your previous convictions are the right ones."

And he should know, since he had sat as one of my judges in the court of honor—not in the first one, when I was discharged after having been already sentenced by a court-martial because of preparation for high treason. (I first heard of the two verdicts in Asturia, where they were useful to me.) No, I am thinking of the second court of honor, though even the word "honor" belongs to those terms which have become thoroughly suspect.

So I was rehabilitated by people like Twinnings, who, wisely, had been living with his English relatives. By rights, it was he who should have had to justify himself. Something else strange: in my records the verdict is still listed. Governments change, files remain. The paradox remained: in the dossiers of the State the fact that I had risked my neck for it was simultaneously listed forever as treason. When my name was mentioned, the exalted file clerks in the government offices, who sat on their chairs only because I and people like me allowed them to, made a wry face.

Apart from this significant item, I admit that a few other trifles were listed also in my papers. Among them was one of those pranks we think up when we feel high-spirited—it hap-, pened when we still had a monarchy. "The desecration of a monument" was listed—a time-honored phrase in periods when monuments are no longer monuments. We had toppled over a concrete block with a name on it; I have forgotten which name. To begin with, we were a little drunk, and secondly, nothing is easier to forget nowadays than both the names which, only yesterday, were the talk of the town and the notables after whom the streets were named. The eagerness to erect monuments in their honor is extraordinary and, more often than not, hardly outlasts their lifetime.

All this not only damaged my reputation but had been entirely unnecessary. I didn't like to think of it now. But others had a remarkable memory.

Well, Twinnings seemed to think that my former convictions had been the right ones. On the other hand, I didn't like the idea that Zapparoni might also consider them the right ones. For what would that mean? It would mean that he was looking for someone with, as it were, two handles: not only a solid one which can be grasped, but another one too. He needed someone who was solid but not through and through.

A popular proverb calls the kind of factotum required in this case, a person "with whom you can steal horses." This expression perhaps had its origin in times when the stealing of horses was risky but not disreputable. If it came off well, the affair was creditable; if not, you were hanged from the willow tree or forfeited your ears.

The adage was fairly apposite to my situation. There was, of course, a slight difference: although Zapparoni was evidently looking for a man with whom he could "steal horses," he himself was far too important a person to go on a scouting trip with him. But what could I do? There was still another proverb applicable to my situation: that the devil puts up with flies when he has nothing else to eat. So I said to Twinnings: "Well, I shall try, if you think I should. Perhaps he'll take me.

But, just between old comrades, I'll tell you: I refuse to get involved in anything shady."

Twinnings set me at ease. After all, I was not applying for a job with just any odd person but with a firm of world-wide repute. He would call Zapparoni this very day and would let me know. I had a chance. Twinnings rang the bell, and Frederick appeared.

Frederick, too, had grown older; he walked with a slight stoop, and the bald patch on his head was encircled by a thin, snowy-white fringe. I still knew him from the good old days, when he took care of Twinnings' uniform. If you visited Twinnings you always met Frederick in the anteroom; usually he had in his hands an instrument, now antiquated and only fit for a museum, called a buttonhole scissors. Incidentally, whatever opinion you may have arrived at concerning a man like Twinnings, the fact that a valet sticks to his job with him for decades, is a plus for his master.

When Frederick entered the room, his face lit up with a smile. It was a wonderful moment, this moment of harmony, uniting the three of us. A glimmer of our carefree youth came back in a flash. Good God, how the world had changed since then! I sometimes thought that this sentiment had something to do with getting older. Each generation, after all, looks back on the good old days. But in our case it was something quite different, something horribly different. Of course, differences existed between military service under Henry IV, Louis XIII, or Louis XIV, but one always served on horseback. Today these magnificent creatures were doomed. They had disappeared from the fields and streets, from the villages and towns, and for years they had not been seen in combat. Everywhere they had been replaced by automatons. Corresponding to this change was a change in men: they became more mechanical, more calculable, and often you hardly felt that you were among human beings. Only at rare moments did I still hear a sound from the past—the sound of bugles at sunrise and the neighing of horses, which made our hearts tremble. All that has gone.

Twinnings ordered breakfast: toast, ham and eggs, port, other things. All his life he had breakfasted heartily; often the sign of positive natures. He had suffered much less from the hardships of the times than I and many others had. Without making great compromises, people like Twinnings are useful everywhere; they make light of any government. They take things only as seriously and importantly as is necessary: a change in circumstances goes only skin-deep with them. He had been one of the judges at my trial. It was my destiny that those for whom I had taken risks passed judgment upon me.

He filled my glass with port. I washed down my resentment. "Here's to you, old Mercurian."

He laughed. "When you work for Zapparoni, you won't lead a dog's life either. We'll call Teresa at once."

"Very kind of you to think of it—but she went out shopping."

Why didn't I tell him that, together with all the rest, they had disconnected our telephone. It probably wouldn't be news to him. He certainly knew, cunning fox that he was, that I had an empty stomach. But he had not ordered breakfast until I agreed.

After all that has been said, surely nobody has gained the impression that Twinnings went to all this trouble gratuitously. The only exception he made with former comrades was that they did not have to pay him a commission. But, of course, he compensated himself. To men like Zapparoni, a few pounds did not matter.

Twinnings was doing well in his business. The advantage of it was that it hardly looked like a business. It consisted in his knowing a lot of people and profiting thereby. I, too, knew many people, but this did not help my economics; I had even more expenses. But Twinnings knew Zapparoni and myself: it meant business for him. Moreover, it was easy work; no one else I knew had a more pleasant and regular mode of life. He did business while he was breakfasting, dining, and when he went to the theater in the evening. There are people to whom money flows easily and inconspicuously; they do not know the difficulties others have. As long as I had known Twinnings, he had been one of these, and he had not changed. Even his parents had been well-to-do.

I don't want to put him in too unfavorable a light; everyone has his weaknesses and his strengths. Twinnings, for example, did not have to do what now occurred to him—go into the next room, and return with a fifty-pound note, which he handed to me. I needed little persuasion to accept it.

Beyond any doubt he did not want me to show up at Zapparoni's completely broke. But yet another matter underlay this gesture—our old comradeship. It was Monteron's training, which no one who had ever received it could belie. How often had we cursed him, lying dog-tired on our beds after a day when one drill had followed on the heels of another—on foot, on horseback, in the stables, and on the endless sandy tracks. Monteron recognized these moments of despair and took a delight in capping it all with some night drill—for instance, an alert.

I have to admit that the lazy flesh disappeared. Our muscles became hard as steel, refined on the anvil of an experienced blacksmith. Even our faces changed. Among other things, we learned to ride, to fence, to take a fall. And these we learned for life. On our characters, too, Monteron left his permanent mark. He could become especially disagreeable when he heard that one of us had left a comrade in a tight spot. If a drunken cadet had got into a scrape, Monteron's first question was: Was anyone with him? And God have mercy on the fellow who had abandoned his comrade and who had not looked after him as though he were a small child. That you must never, under any circumstances, leave a comrade alone in danger—whether in the city or in combat—was one of the basic principles which Monteron hammered into our heads, either at the sandbox or during the field exercises or on those formidable Mondays.

Although we were a lightheaded bunch of youths, in this regard he was successful—nobody can deny that. When we were gathered around him on the evening before we joined our regiments—he became very genial and gay—our dinner was more than an ordinary farewell gathering. He would perhaps say: "There has been no shining light in this year's class, and in other respects it has been hard work. But there is not one of you on whom the King could not rely. That is, after all, the main point."

None of us drank too much that evening. We clearly understood that something more than the King, more than his office, stood behind the Old Man; this knowledge remained with us for life and perhaps even longer. It lasted even when no one any longer remembered who the King had been. Monteron, too, was long since forgotten—actually, ours had been the last class he had charge of. He was among the first to be killed—before Liège, I believe, at night. Of his pupils, too, only a few are alive.

But you could still recognize his stamp on all of us. Later we used to meet once or twice a year in the backroom of small eating places, in the middle of cities so strangely changed, having been twice destroyed and rebuilt in the meanwhile. On these evenings Monteron's name inevitably came up in our talk as through curtains of flame, and the atmosphere of that farewell celebration, of that last evening, was for a moment recaptured.

Once Monteron had said: "Twinnings, you are really more 'light' than 'cavalryman' "—stinging words indeed; but even on such a businessman, Monteron had left his distinctive mark. I am convinced that Twinnings acted against his true nature when, seeing me sit at his table like a poor relative, he went into the next room to fetch me some spending money. But, after having forced me to swallow a bitter pill, he could not act otherwise, for Monteron was reawakened in him. Twinnings remembered one of the basic patterns which Monteron had stamped on our minds, namely, that I stood in the front line—though it was not a respectable one—and he in the reserve.

So we were agreed, and Twinnings walked me to the door. Then something else flashed into my mind:

"And who had this job up to now?"·

"Another Italian, Caretti; but he left three months ago."

"Retired?"

"Something like that. Never heard of again, vanished into space, and nobody knows where he is now."

III

This conversation took place on a Saturday. On Monday morning I took a taxi out to the plant. On Saturday evening Twinnings had given me an affirmative answer. At Zapparoni's they worked, of course, on Sundays.

Teresa had put my things in order. She was overjoyed by the news and immediately saw me in a high position; she had made up a fantasy for herself. She had much too high an opinion of me; she probably needed it. Timid about herself, she was convinced that she was a drag on me, a burden damaging to my career. The opposite was true. If, in this increasingly dismal world, I still had something like a home, it was with her.

When we were in trouble—and this was the rule recently—I often felt at night, beside me, that almost inperceptible trembling of a woman who wants to conceal her weeping. When I urged her to tell me the reason, she always told the same story: first, that it would have been much better had she never been born and that she and I had never met; then, that she had spoiled my career and ruined me. It did no good to tell her that I had always been man enough to ruin myself without help; in fact, that my greatest success came in just this—but I could not talk her out of her absurd ideas.

We derive, it's true, a certain moral support from being overrated. It stimulates the good in us. As I've said before, I was used to this sort of thing from my mother, whose image, incidentally, as I held it in my memory, had fused imperceptibly with that of Teresa. How often, during the frequent stormy scenes at home, had my mother sided with me against my father. She would say: "But our boy is not a bad boy," to which my father retorted: "He is and always will be a good-for-nothing." Then mother would say again: "But bad he definitely is not,"—because a woman must always have the last word.

The Zapparoni plant was some distance outside the city. In almost every town there were large and small affiliated establishments—branches and licensed firms, warehouses, replacement and repair shops—but this plant was the head, the master workshop for the models, from which year by year novel and miraculous surprises flooded the world as if poured from a cornucopia. Here Zapparoni himself lived when he was not traveling.

Twinnings' telegram had arrived on Saturday: I was to come for an interview. On Sunday since I was haunted by what Twinnings had told me before I had left, I succeeded

in running to earth Caretti's family doctor. The consultation
had set me at ease. The doctor did not think he was betray-
ing a confidence when he told me what had been the matter
with Caretti; in any case it was generally known. Like so
many overscrupulous people at Zapparoni's, Caretti had gradually become peculiar, eventually beyond the admissible limit.
A manic disturbance, diagnosed by the doctors as a compul-
sion neurosis coupled with a persecution mania, was nourished
by hallucinations about automatons. In such cases the patients
believe themselves threatened by cunningly devised machinery, and their world slowly transforms itself into a phantas-
magoria, similar to the imaginings of medieval painters. Caretti had suffered from the delusion of being encircled by
minute, evilly-intentioned airplanes.

It is not unusual that such disturbed people disappear and
never turn up again. The doctor, a slightly built, nervous
psychiatrist, remembered a patient whose remains had been
found after some years in a badger's burrow: he had crawled
into it and killed himself. The doctor was very voluble, de-
scribing the symptoms pedantically but with such relish that
on my way home I almost reached the point of imagining myself threatened by similar phantoms. Actually, I was much
relieved.

The plant now appeared in the distance: low white towers
and flat-roofed ateliers in great numbers, all without antennas
or chimneys. The buildings were surrounded by bright
colors, since the all-encircling wall was covered with innumerable posters. A side line of the business, cultivated by
Zapparoni with special devotion, was the cinema, which he
had brought to an almost fabulous perfection with his robots
and automatons.

Prognoses which have been made contend that our technology will terminate in pure necromancy. If so, everything we
now experience would be only a departure and mechanics
would become refined to a degree that would no longer

require any crude embodiment. Lights, words, yes even thoughts, would be sufficient. Clearly, the Zapparoni films had very nearly realized such a future. The dreams of old Utopians were coarse-grained in comparison. With the freedom and elegance of dancers, the automatons had opened up a world of their own. Here a principle operative only in dreams—namely, that matter thinks—seemed to be realized. Naturally, these movies had a strong attraction. Children, in particular, were held spellbound. Zapparoni had dethroned the old stock figures of the fairy tales. Like one of the storytellers who sits down on a carpet in an Arabian coffeehouse and transforms the room, he spun out his fables. He created novels which could not only be read, heard, and seen but could be entered as one enters a garden. In his opinion, nature was inadequate, both in its beauty and logic, and should be surpassed. He created, in fact, a style which became a model for the actors who adapted themselves to it. Among his creations were the most charming puppets—truly enchanting visions.

These movies had contributed to Zapparoni's popularity in a very special way. He had become the kind grandfather who tells stories. One thought of him as having a long white beard like an old-fashioned Santa Claus. Parents even complained that their children were too preoccupied with him. They could not fall asleep, were overexcited, had nightmares. But after all, life was a strain everywhere. Pressure molded the race, and one had to put up with it.

Advertisements for such movies completely covered the wall which enclosed the plant on all four sides. And a street, so wide that it resembled the approach to a fortification, ran around its whole length. Without the colorful posters, the wall would, undoubtedly, have looked too sober, too much like a fortress, chiefly because of the pale towers which rose above it at intervals. Over the whole complex of buildings a yellow balloon floated.

Along the road, bright signs indicated that we were entering a restricted area. The driver dutifully called my attention to them. We had to drive slowly and were not permitted to carry either weapons, or Geiger counters, or cameras, binoculars, etc. Protective suits and sunglasses were also prohibited. There was a lively traffic both on the road and around the wall; the byways, on the other hand, were completely empty.

Gradually the posters became more distinct. They depicted the visit of Heinz-Otto to the Queen of the Termites: Tannhäuser in Venusberg, adapted to a child's mind. Here Zapparoni's robots appeared as rich and powerful gnomes: the splendor and the marvels of her subterranean palace no longer showed the slightest trace of artificiality. This type of movie ran in twelve chapters through the whole calendar year and children were consumed with curiosity about each episode. This serial influenced their way of dressing and their tastes. You could see them in the playgrounds—now as space travelers, now as speleologists, another time as sailors in submarines or as cowboys. With these technically-tinged fairy tales and adventure stories, Zapparoni aroused strong and lasting enthusiasm. The children lived in his world. Parents and teachers were of two minds: some felt that children learned easily from them, while others were afraid that they might become too excited. And it is true that strange and alarming effects were often observed. But you cannot stop the trend of the times. In any case, is the real world any less fantastic? What *doesn't* overstimulate children?

We turned into the employees' parking lot. Compared to their limousines, my hired cab looked like a crow that had strayed among pheasants. I paid the driver and set off for the reception desk. Although it was midmorning, the traffic was lively at the main entrance. The best proof that Zapparoni's workers were actually masters was the fact that they kept no hours. They came and went as they pleased, provided they were not working on a team—which was exceptional in the workshop for models. As a matter of fact, this regulation or rather non-regulation had advantages for Zapparoni. His personnel policies left nothing to be desired; work was done after the fashion of artists who are obsessed with their creation. No time limit existed—so work went on almost continuously. The workmen dreamed of their works of art. That they were their own bosses was evident from the fact that they had time of their own. But this did not mean that they wasted it. They possessed time in the way rich men possess money. The rich man's wealth is founded on his purse, and not on his manner of spending money. You sense his wealth by the way he carries himself.

Those who entered and left the plant wore white or colored laboratory coats and passed through the gate without any ceremony. One could conclude from this that they were well known, for the gate, which was also the entry to the reception office, was closely guarded by small groups which stood around as if receiving passengers on an ocean liner. As these newcomers cross the gangplank, they are faced by sailors, stewards, and other ship's personnel, who watch them closely and discreetly. The entrance in this case was wide and low. On either side of the corridor were doors—I read "Reception," "Caretaker," "Guard," and other signs.

At the reception desk they seemed to expect me. As soon as I mentioned my name, a page boy stepped forward. He had been waiting for me.

To my surprise, instead of leading me into the factory he led me back through the gate to a small underground station which opened off the parking lot. After descending into it, we stepped into a very small car, which stood on rails and was operated like a self-service elevator. In two minutes we had reached our goal. We stopped in front of an old-fashioned building within a walled park. I was standing before Zapparoni's private residence.

The most I had expected was to be taken to the employment office and from there—should my application, thanks to Twinnings' recommendation, be well received—perhaps to the chief of personnel himself. It took my breath away, therefore, when, emerging from the earth, I suddenly found myself before the Holy of Holies, in the sphere of a man who—some people contended—did not exist at all but was perhaps the most cunning invention of the Zapparoni Works. A servant came down the stairs and took me over from the page boy. "Mr. Zapparoni is expecting you," he said.

There was no possible doubt; I was in the residence of Zapparoni. Formerly his principal factory had been situated elsewhere, until, tired of the constant need to alter and add to the buildings, he had decided to bring the plant, newly designed, to that degree of perfection which distinguished all his creations, whether large or small. When they inspected the new building site, they discovered a Cistercian abbey in the vicinity. For many years now it had been public property, but was rarely used. The church and the main building had fallen victims to time, but the monastery wall and the refectory were intact. Apart from the monks' large dining hall, the refectory building contained still other rooms which had once served as kitchens, store- and guestrooms. This building Zapparoni had taken over and made his home. The house had imposing proportions. Now and then, I had seen reproductions of it in illustrated magazines.

The large gate in the monastery wall was always locked; the people who lived in the house and any guests came and went by the little underground train. It had struck me that I had not boarded the train at a terminal. Most likely, it ran not only to the parking lot, but also into the plant.

Thus Zapparoni didn't need to leave his own grounds, and a strict control of all visitors was possible. In this way the master of the house was protected against the impudence of reporters and particularly of photographers. His person and his habits he carefully kept in semi-obscurity, since he was aware of the wearing and consuming force of publicity. He wanted to be talked about a great deal, but only vaguely and allusively. (In the same way, his contraptions were meant to give the impression that their visible parts were by far the least important.) The selection of published pictures and reports was made by himself and his experts.

His director of public relations had developed a system of indirect *reportage* which stimulated but never quite satisfied curiosity. A famous person whose face one does not know is generally thought of as being handsome and imposing. A person who is much discussed but whose residence is unknown is suspected of being everywhere—he seems to multiply himself miraculously. A person so powerful that one does not even dare speak of him becomes almost omnipresent, since he dominates our inner life. We imagine that he overhears our conversations and that his eyes rest on us in our closest and most private moments. A name that is only whispered is more powerful than one shouted from the rooftops. All this Zapparoni knew. On the other hand he could not ignore publicity completely. This fact introduced mystifying surprises into his propaganda. It was a new system.

I cannot deny that I was gripped with fear when I heard the servant say: "Mr. Zapparoni is expecting you." I felt the crass disproportion between one of the mighty of the earth and a man who had scarcely enough money in his pocket to pay his fare home. All at once I was overcome by the feeling that I was not equal to this confrontation. It was a sign that I was, in fact, on the downgrade—a feeling that I had never known before. Monteron had often told us that, under no circumstances, was a cavalryman allowed to indulge in this feeling. He would also say: "Only when the captain leaves the ship is the ship lost and derelict. The true captain goes down with his ship."

All this went through my mind while my knees trembled.

I also thought of the times, long ago, when movies and automatons did not yet exist for us—except perhaps at the annual fairs—and we had looked down our noses at those steel, textile, and coal tycoons. A small landowner with two-hundred acres, whose sleep was troubled by the thought of his debts, was more easily accepted by the Light Cavalry than those fellows who drove the first automobiles which made the horses shy. The horses sensed what was in store for them. Since then the world had changed.

Because Zapparoni was taking the time to receive me personally, I concluded that he thought I could be a partner. This thought stung me. Could I really be a partner in some regular business? If, for example, a poor girl gets a job with a big firm, where she has to keep the files in order, take shorthand or type, she may never see the head of the firm face to face. She is not his partner. But should she someday be seen with him on the beach or in a night club, she would grow in importance while, at the same time, losing respect. She would then have become an irregular partner as a consequence of entering into a power relationship. On the legitimate side she would have become weak, but on the illegitimate, strong.

Zapparoni's reception of me in his private residence—me, the hungry, discharged cavalryman—put me in a similar situation. He could not make a great show of me. Neither in his offices nor in his workshops could I be of any use. And even if I could handle these positions brilliantly, he would scarcely make a personal effort to get hold of me. Clearly, therefore, he was expecting something different of me—some work which one doesn't imagine everybody capable of or wanting to do.

With these thoughts in mind, I felt very much like taking to my heels, although I was already halfway up the stairs. But there was Teresa, there were my debts, there was my hopeless situation. Most likely he required a man in just this kind of fix. If I turned back now, I would regret it.

And there was something else. Why should I pretend to be a better man than I am? Monteron scarcely ever occupied himself with philosophy—unless one wants to consider Clausewitz a philosopher—but he liked to quote as one of his favorite maxims: "There are, once and for all, matters I do not wish to know." His predilection for this maxim betrayed a straightforward singleness of mind, without subterfuges or bypaths. The phrase, "to understand is to forgive," did not exist for him. Both the master and the moralist are revealed in restraint.

Although I learned and adopted a great deal from Monteron, in this respect I never followed his example. On the contrary, there are very few things into which I haven't poked my nose. But you cannot change your nature. My father had often reproached me for this. When we were dining out, for example, and he handed me the menu, he would say: "Isn't it strange that the boy always selects the most unusual dishes, though the ordinary menu is excellent."

He was right: the restaurant offered a good bill of fare. The cadets used to dine there. But the menu was boring. I studied it carefully, looking for bamboo sprouts and Indian birds' nests. Father then relented and only said to my mother: "He cannot have inherited it from me."

He was right as always (my mother had good and simple tastes too). In any case, it is doubtful whether such idiosyncrasies are inheritable. I rather think that they are drawn like prizes in a lottery.

To go back to the menu: the dishes I selected on account of their names usually were a disappointment. Later on, when traveling, I had the same experience with exotic delicacies and stimulants. I rarely let them pass. Houses of ill-repute and bars, sinister streets and neighborhoods, obscene antique shops also attracted me. And it was hard to resist the type who beckoned me to follow him into a dark doorway on Montmartre with the intention of leading me to his sister. This

would not have been unusual if, at the same time, I had not
felt a strong aversion to these situations. But my curiosity got
the upper hand. Yet I was never satisfied; in the same way that
I choked over those distasteful and strangely named dishes, so
the sight of human degradation could not satisfy me. Vice left
a melancholy, painful, and lasting memory. This explains why
it never got a hold on me. Yet I am still puzzled why I
searched for it again and again. Only after I met Teresa did I
learn that a handful of water gives more strength than any
magic potion.

Incidentally, my curiosity was sometimes an asset to me,
for a cavalryman's chief task is reconnaissance. When patrol-
ling an unsafe terrain, I frequently reconnoitered far beyond
what was necessary and ordered. This led to unsuspected dis-
coveries, and the front-line officers were impressed. Well,
there is no defect without its own virtue and vice versa.

In short, on Zapparoni's staircase I felt that I was ventur-
ing upon an ambiguous adventure, though from necessity.
My old fatal curiosity, however, stirred again and goaded me
on. I was itching to hear what the Old Man had up his
sleeve, and why he had condescended to take an interest in
me. Curiosity provoked me almost more strongly than the
prospect of profit. After all, hadn't I often wriggled my head
out of the noose, and hadn't I frequently nibbled the bait
without getting hooked?

So I followed the servant into the old house which gave
the impression of a country seat. The entrance led into a hall-
way where not only hats and coats but fowling pieces and
fishing tackle were kept. Then we came into a large hall, two
stories high, hung with trophies and with engravings by Ried-
erer. Two or three additional chambers followed, larger than
a room but smaller than a hall.

All the rooms were on the south side of the house, and the
sunshine, subdued by the opaque window panes, filtered down
upon the carpets. I was shown into the library. At first sight

all of the furniture seemed within the means of any well-to-do person, and it did not come up to my expectations. Influenced by newspaper reports, I had expected to see a kind of magician's study, where the visitor is partly amazed and partly nonplussed by mechanical surprises. In this I saw at once I had been completely mistaken. Of course I should have guessed that a magician and lord of automatons would not want that sort of thing in the privacy of his home. Certainly, we all relax in ways as utterly different from our occupations as possible. A general will hardly play with toy soldiers and a mailman will not willingly march for miles on a Sunday. It is also said that clowns are almost always grave, if not melancholy, within their four walls.

Here, one's eyes were not hurt by the bad taste of the furnishings, as in rooms of the newly rich. There was no display of wealth in the manner of Trimalchio. Zapparoni must not only have employed an excellent interior decorator but must be a man of taste himself. The style of the furnishings showed this. Harmony such as this cannot be made to order; it is created by an inner need, by the character of the man who had made this his home. Here was no chilling splendor, no wish merely to show off; the rooms were inhabited by an intelligent and cultivated human being who felt at home in them.

Natives of southern countries—they may come from a Sicilian village or be the descendants of a Neapolitan basso—frequently possess a taste as infallible as that handed down by long family tradition. They have an unerring ear for melody and, in the fine arts, an incorruptible eye for the hand of the master. I had often observed this. The only danger lies in their vanity.

The whole house bore the mark of sensible moderation: it was not pompous but radiated a breath of life. This was especially noticeable in the works of art. On occasion I'd had the chance to see famous paintings and sculpture, otherwise known only from calendars or museums, in the houses of men who had recently come into wealth or power. The sight of these works had been disappointing, because they had lost their expression and their language, just as birds, imprisoned in a cage, forfeit their song and their brilliance. A work of art wastes away and becomes lusterless in surroundings where it has a price but not a value. It radiates only when surrounded by love. It is bound to wilt in a world where the rich have no time and the cultivated no money. But it never harmonizes with borrowed greatness.

Zapparoni, however—I saw that in passing—obviously had time. The five or six paintings which hung on the walls impressed me as objects upon which their owner's eye rested daily with love. None of them could have been painted after 1750. Among them was a Poussin. They all gave off a breath of peace, and disclaimed any effect. By this I do not mean the effect of modern painters, who limit themselves to pure invention, but the effect produced by masters. These paintings, assembled here by Zapparoni, could never have seemed surprising, not even to their contemporaries. From the very beginning they must have seemed familiar.

This impression, transmitted to the entire house, was linked with another impression, concerning the problem of pure power, and was intensified by it. As I said before, we live in times when words have lost or changed their meaning and have become ambiguous. This also holds true for the word "house," formerly the very essence of stability and permanence. For some time now a house has become a sort of tent, but without giving the freedom enjoyed by nomads. Buildings are pushed up high, and jerry-built structures rise by the thousands. This would not be so bad if, at least for a short while, one could feel safe in one's own and untouchable home. The opposite is true: today the man who has the courage to build himself a house constructs a meeting place for the people who will descend upon him on foot, by car, or by telephone. Employees of the gas, the electric, and of the waterworks will arrive; agents of life and fire insurance companies; building inspectors, collectors of the radio tax; mortgage creditors and rent assessors who tax you for living in your own home.

When the political climate grows harsher, quite different people turn up and know at once where to find you. In addition to these nuisances, the odium of being a proprietor clings to you.

It was easier in the old days. Even though you had fewer conveniences, you felt at peace when you stretched your legs under your own table. This was the very feeling I had about Zapparoni, namely, that he was still master in his own house. I could have bet that no gas meters or other connections existed here, at least not the kind that lead out of the premises. Probably Zapparoni had transferred the pattern of a feudal state to his household, and his automatons had enabled him to do this. In the automaton, abstract power becomes concrete and returns into the object. I noticed nothing of this directly; it was more a question of atmospheric perception. Candles stood on the table and there was even an hourglass on the mantelpiece.

Quite obviously, the person who lived here did not live on a pension; he distributed pensions. Here no police could intrude, no matter what the order or what the pretext. Not only did Zapparoni have his own police to carry out his, and only his, instructions, but the whole plant and its connecting roads were guarded by policemen and engineers of State and Army, who, true to the letter, had to act with him "in agreement," but actually could have no opinion of their own.

The question, of course, arises: why was a man with such prerogatives dependent upon me, of all people—someone up to his neck in difficulties. Here lay that mystery of which I have already spoken. The fact is—and it must be a strange, deeply-rooted one—that a person, however many legal methods of action he has at his disposal, is still dependent on loop-

holes for carrying out his plans. The legal sphere, small or
large, always borders upon the illegal one. The borderline ad-
vances with the prerogatives. For that reason transgressions
are found more frequently among those on top than among
those on the bottom. When prerogatives become absolute,
the frontiers tend to blur, and it is difficult to distinguish between right and wrong. At this point people are needed with
whom one can "steal horses."

I V

After the servant had shown me into the library, he left me
alone. He had behaved with the utmost politeness. I mention
this because it shows how suspicious I had become. I had come
to watch everyone I met, and was much more quickly hurt
than I used to be. In any case, I could draw no conclusion
from the behavior of the servant: perhaps his master had made
a derogatory remark concerning my visit; perhaps not. Well, I
still doubted that I would meet Zapparoni face to face—one
of his secretaries would probably enter at any moment.

It was peaceful in the library. The books gave the room a
quiet dignity. They lined the shelves in bindings of light
parchment, flamed vellum, and brown morocco. The vol-
umes bound in parchment were inscribed by hand; the leath-
erbacks bore red and green labels or had their titles printed in

gold. In spite of its age, the collection of books did not give the impression of being there as decoration. I examined a few titles—early technical treatises, books on the cabala, Rosicrucianism, and alchemy—but they didn't tell me much. Perhaps in such books a mind could relax reading about the ancient false trails.

The thick walls would have made the room gloomy, had not the high windows, which almost reached to the floor, let in a flood of light. The French doors were open; and led out onto a large terrace.

Looking out over the park was like looking at an old painting. The trees sparkled in the brilliance of their fresh foliage; the eye sensed their roots drawing moisture from deep down in the soil. They formed a border along the little brook, which ran lazily, at times widening into pools which glistened with a green coat of algae. These had once been the fishponds of the monks; the Cistercians had built in the marshland like beavers.

It was a piece of luck that the wall was still intact. In the vicinity of cities, these rings of stone have generally been demolished and now serve as quarries. But now and then one saw here the gray stone showing through the leaves of the trees. The wall even seemed to enclose a field, since in the distance I could see a peasant walking behind his plow. The air was clear; the sun glinted on the coats of the horses and on the clods which were broken up by the plowshare. It was an idyllic picture, although a surprising one to find on the premises of a man who, among other things, dealt in tractors which loosened the topsoil of flowerbeds like moles. But everything in his household clearly indicated museum tendencies. Most likely he did not want to see machines when, from his terrace, he looked at his trees and ponds. There was the additional advantage that only garden produce grown in the old manner appeared on his table. Here, the saying that words have changed is still valid, since bread is no longer bread and wine no longer wine. They are doubtful chemicals. At present one really has to be unusually rich to avoid being poisoned. No doubt about it: this man Zapparoni was a sly fox who understood how to live in his *Malpertuis*—and at the expense of fools. He was like the pharmacist who asks the most exorbitant prices for his pills and miracle-drugs, while he, himself, keeps in good health as his forefathers did.

No doubt, there was peace in this place. The steady roar of the plant, the rumble from the parking lot and the driveways reached me only as a low murmur across the treetops. I could, on the other hand, hear the melodies of the blackbirds and finches, and the woodpecker rap with its beak against rotting tree trunks. Thrushes hopped and lingered on the lawns, and now and then the plop of a leaping carp could be heard from the ponds. On the flower-crowded borders and medallions in front of the terrace, bees crossed to and fro, sharing with the butterflies the sweet loot. It was a May day in its full glory.

After I had examined the paintings and the books with their odd titles, I sat down on one of the two chairs which stood by a small table, and gazed through the wide-open door. The air was purer here than in the city and almost intoxicating. The eye rested on the old trees, the green ponds, and on the brown field in the distance, where the peasant made his furrows, turning his plow about at the end of each.

Just as we still feel the winter in our bones on a warm day in spring, I felt, before this vista, the deep discontent which had clouded my life in these last years. A retired cavalryman cuts a poor figure in the middle of these cities, where the neighing of a horse is no longer heard. How things had changed since Monteron's death! Words had lost their meaning; even war was no longer war. Monteron would turn in his grave if he could hear what they called war nowadays. After all, peace was no longer peace.

Two or three times more, we were to ride our horses on the plains where, ever since the Great Migration of the Peoples, armed horsemen had moved, time and again. Soon we were to learn that this was no longer possible. We had proudly worn our handsome and colorful uniforms, which could be seen glittering from a distance, but we could no longer see our opponent. Marksmen, invisible to us, took aim at long range and unhorsed us. If we managed to reach them, we found them within a web of wires which cut through the fetlocks of the horses and was impossible to jump. This was the end of the cavalry. We had to dismount.

In the tanks it was close, hot, and noisy, as if one sat in a boiler on which steamfitters hammered. It smelled of oil, gasoline, rubber, scorched insulating tape, asbestos and—should we come into the firing zone—of powder, which puffed out of the cartridges. We felt concussions in the soft ground, then sharper and nearer impacts, then direct hits. These were not the great days of the cavalry, which Monteron had described to us, but hot machinework, obscure and without glory, always accompanied by the prospect of death by fire. I was repulsed by the thought that the spirit should in this manner submit itself to the power of flame—a deep-seated natural feeling.

Naturally our profession took on a disreputable character. Soon I recognized that soldiers were no longer soldiers. The distrust was mutual and the whole service was affected. Formerly, the pledge to the flag had sufficed; now it became necessary to enlist numerous policemen. This was a disturbing change. What once had been duty became, overnight, an error or even a crime. We noticed this when, after the war had been lost, we returned to our homeland. Words had lost their meaning—should fatherland no longer be fatherland? For what, then, had they all died—Monteron and the others?

This question weighed on all our minds. We began to brood but didn't find a solution. Apparently our education, though severe, had been too narrow. We didn't understand the simplest matter. It is indisputable, for example, that of two warring armies one is bound to lose, unless it comes to a draw.

But that defeat had fallen to *our* lot was too much for us. We couldn't assimilate it; somewhere within us there must have been a blind spot. Although it was obvious and palpable, we did not accept our defeat.

We could not have been more wrong. We should have swallowed and digested defeat like a bitter medicine. Instead we began to convince ourselves that only treason could have caused our downfall, and that we had been defeated contrary to the rules of the game. This was bound to lead us on a wrong track.

I do not like to think of those years when everything had changed; I should like to wipe them out of my memory like a bad dream. Everyone suspected everyone else. When hate is in the seeds, you can only harvest weeds.

A horrible incident made me sick of all intrigues. It happened at the time when we had overturned the monument that had been erected for one of the new tribunes who already had become unpopular. ("Tribune" is one of those words based on the fact that there once was a Roman Empire.) We had been drinking; it was past midnight, and the monument stood in the glaring lights of a building site. The workmen lent us their pickaxes, and we did such a thorough job that we left only two huge boots of concrete looming up from the pedestal. I only vaguely remember the place and the names of my companions in this obscure iconoclastic sacrilege; whoever might take an interest in it, as Zapparoni perhaps did, can look it up in my papers.

We used to meet in the room of a comrade who lived on the top floor of one of those tenements which were being built quickly and badly. The room had one large window, from which one looked down, as through a deep shaft, into the courtyard which, from this height, appeared not much larger than a playing card. This comrade's name was Lorenz, a slender, slightly nervous fellow who had also served in the Light Cavalry. We all liked him; there was an air of the old freedom and ease about him. In those days almost everyone was possessed with an idea: this was a peculiarity of the years following that war. Lorenz' idea consisted in seeing the machine as the source of all evil. Therefore, he intended to blow up the factories, to redistribute the land, to transform the country into a large peasant commune in which everyone would be peaceful, healthy, and happy. In substantiation of his opinion, he had assembled a small library—two or three shelves full of well-thumbed books, chiefly by Tolstoy, who was his saint.

The poor boy did not know that at present there is only one kind of land reform: expropriation. Indeed, he himself was the son of an expropriated farmer who had not survived his losses. Oddest of all, Lorenz advocated these ideas on the top floor of a tenement, in the midst of a group which, if not lacking in confused schemes, was, at least in technical matters, up-to-date.

As a result, he was constantly interrupted as he developed his ideas: "Back to the Stone Age," we'd mock, or, "Neanderthal, I love you." But we overlooked, or failed to recognize, that our friend was consumed with something like a holy if helpless wrath; for life in these burnt-out cities, which smoldered as if gutted by metallic beaks, was ghastly. Lorenz shouldn't have been in our rowdy company; in those days he should have been in the care of a family or a wife who loved him. Monteron had been especially fond of him.

On that terrible evening—it was actually almost early morning—we had been drinking heavily, and our heads were flushed with excitement. Empty bottles stood along the walls, and from the ash trays wreaths of smoke drifted out the open window, through which one saw a sickly sky. All this was far removed from the peace of villages. ·

I was half-asleep and only the noise of the conversation kept me awake. Suddenly I gave a start; I felt that something was taking place in the room that called for the utmost attention. In the same way, a receiving instrument starts to vibrate when a message is transmitted and music is interrupted by the distress signals of a ship in danger of sinking.

My comrades had stopped talking; they were looking at Lorenz who had risen from his chair in extreme agitation. Perhaps they had been teasing him again, treating as a joke a condition that called for an experienced doctor. Only later did they realize how unusual all this had been.

Since Lorenz was a teetotaler, it was obvious that he was not drunk but in a sort of trance. He no longer defended his idea; instead, he complained about the lack of men of good will—his plans could be so easily realized if only such men existed. Our fathers had set an example. It would be so easy to consummate the sacrifice which the times expected from us. Only when it was consummated would the crack which split the world in two be closed.

We looked at him, not understanding what he was driving at; at one moment we felt like spectators of a senseless tirade, at the next like witnesses to an incantation in which something uncanny flickered up.

He became quieter, as if weighing in his mind a particularly convincing phrase. He smiled and repeated: "But it's so easy. I'll show you." Then he shouted: "Long live——" and jumped out of the window.

I shall not repeat the name he spoke. We thought we were dreaming, but at the same time we felt as though we were connected by an electric current; we sat in the suddenly empty room like an assembly of ghosts, our hair standing on end.

Although the youngest of us, Lorenz had been a leader in gymnastics; I had often seen him vaulting over the parallel bars or the horse. In exactly the same way he disappeared from that attic; he had lightly placed his hand on the window sill and then turned round, so that his face looked once more into the room. Did the great silence which followed last five or seven seconds? I do not know. In any case, even in remembering, one would like to drive a wedge into that inexorable moment, so that it might lose its logic, its inevitability. Then we heard that dreadful, dull, hard thump out of the depth of the courtyard; there was no doubt possible—the fall had been fatal.

We rushed down the stairs and out into the narrow, dim courtyard. I shall not speak about the Thing that huddled in a heap. From such height a body usually lands head first—that Lorenz had managed to land on his feet proved that he had been a good gymnast. From the second, even the third floor, the jump might have been successful. But some things are impossible. I saw two pallid clamps from which hung threadlike shreds: under the impact the thighbones had pierced the hips and now shone white in mid-air.

Someone called for a doctor, another for a pistol, a third for morphine. I felt on the verge of madness and ran away into the night. The tragic act had shocked me deeply and permanently; it had also destroyed something in me. I cannot treat it as just an episode and I cannot dismiss it with the remark that the world is full of senselessness.

Really, doesn't *everything* make sense? There are, of course, things from which we more or less recover, although some of them are too harsh even for saints. But that is no reason to accuse God. Even if there are reasons to doubt him, the fact that he did not arrange the world like a well-ordered parlor is not one of them. It rather speaks in his favor. This used to be much better understood.

As for Lorenz, he did indeed set an example, though different from the one he intended. In one single moment he was able to illustrate and accomplish something which most of our circle took a lifetime to do. If a person of strength and good will who draws his nourishment from the past isn't able to find firm ground under his feet in the present, he is doomed to impotence. If he strives for the impossible, he must destroy himself.

It was then that I fully grasped the terrible words "in vain." After our defeat, I had suffered agonies at the sight of superhuman exploits and immeasurable suffering, above which the words loomed in the red blaze of the night like a rock crowned with vultures. But this incident inflicted a wound which left scars forever.

My comrades apparently took it less seriously. Among the actual participants that night were a number of strong-minded men who, at a later period, were much talked about; it was as if a demon had united them. The next day they met again and decided to cross Lorenz' name from their lists. Suicide was for them an impermissible homage paid to the spirit of the age.

The funeral, held at a suburban cemetery, was a pitiful affair. As the people attending it dispersed, embarrassed remarks could be heard: "Jumped out of the window when drunk," and the like.

V

As for the others, they were soon involved in extraordinary activities. From the Baltic, from Asturia, and from even more remote places, wherever trouble broke out they appeared on the scene. Although they set astonishing things in motion, one could not say that the times encouraged them, except when they were needed to ward off countermoves.

In those years I began to be preoccupied with history. I was curious to learn if anything similar had happened in the past. Among historical characters, I was particularly impressed by the younger Cato, who preferred defeat to victory. To me, as well, it was the recurring shadows in the huge world-canvas which seemed the more impressive, and sadness seemed the true contemplative approach—Hector and Hannibal, the American Indians and the Boers, Montezuma and Maximilian of Mexico. Probably in this interest lay another of the reasons for my failures: misfortune is contagious.

The more active and influential my comrades became, the more they enlisted my assistance. They were good at sizing up potentiality, and in their opinion I was an able instructor. This was true: I had the advantage of being a specialist. But I must modify their view by indicating how far I deserved this title and how far I did not.

There is no doubt that I had a natural gift for teaching, that is for introducing young people to matters which they had been told to learn and must later master. Horsemanship in the *manège*, then in the open country; an intimate understanding of tanks and how to drive them in combat; behavior in fallout zones and other dangerous places—to present information like this methodically, giving both theory and practice, was not difficult for me. I have mentioned once before that my generation was nearly perfect in matters of technology. Whenever I attended a training course in a new invention, you could be sure I'd make the most of it. I even became a member of the board of tank inspectors. We visited factories and bargained with the engineers for their inventions.

These inventions became, incidentally, increasingly revolting to me, for I was ineradicably marked by a touch of the old cavalryman's primitive evaluation. I will admit that in the earliest times the horseman had a considerable advantage over the foot soldier. (On the other hand considerably higher expenses were involved.) But the advantage was balanced by the invention of gunpowder, so rightly lamented by Ariosto. It was the end of glorious armies like those led by Charles the Bold. Cavalry charges still took place of course—and I cannot consider it unjust for the infantryman to load and fire two or three times before he received his comeuppance—but after that, death came to the cavalry.

The old Centaurs were overpowered by the new Titan. I had seen my own conqueror at close hand when I lay bleeding on the grass. He had unhorsed me—a sickly fellow, a pimply lad from the suburbs, some cutler from Sheffield or weaver from Manchester. He cowered behind his rubble heap, one eye shut, the other aiming at me across the machine gun which did the damage. In a pattern of red and gray, he wove an evil cloth. This was the new Polyphemus or, rather, one of his lowest messenger boys with a wire mask before his one-eyed face. This was how the present masters looked. The beauty of the forests was past.

All this puts me in mind of Wittgrewe, one of my first instructors. He taught me the elements of horseback riding, before I came to Monteron. Wittgrewe broke in the new horses, and no riding tournament was conceivable without him. His thighs were hard as iron and his hands, when controlling the reins, were soft as velvet. Within an hour even the most difficult horse, the most untrained colt, recognized him as master. I took part in my first maneuver under his supervision. In the evenings I liked to visit the stables where he had put himself up with his horses. I was in my element there, even if I had been in the saddle all day long, from dawn to the final dismount.

The stables were warm and cozy, and the horses stood belly-deep in the straw. You always met two or three other

Light Cavalrymen with Wittgrewe, all seniors in their third year. There I learned how to take care of my horse after a long ride: how to fill its stall with fresh straw, bringing it water with chaff scattered on top to prevent it from drinking too hastily, how to rub it warm, feeling its fetlocks, nursing it tenderly till it would put its head on my shoulder and nuzzle me with its nose. I was also initiated into the mysteries of the stable-watches which we kept whether we were billeted in a manor or with peasants. I learned to drink schnapps and to smoke a meerschaum, its bowl painted with faces, to play cards and to do the other things which are the ultimate tests of being a soldier. Wherever Wittgrewe appeared, whenever he crossed the farmyard with relaxed, sauntering steps, his coat unbuttoned, the girls soon came from all sides—blondes, brunettes and girls with jet-black hair, girls with pointed shoes or high boots, girls with or without kerchiefs. He took them for granted and did nothing; the girls came like cats when somebody has scattered catnip. They even came into the stable when the peasant and his wife had gone to bed. Then there was much lively drinking, sausages were taken from the larder and cut up, riddles were proposed and favors drawn—in short, Wittgrewe was an all-round man. And he had a splendid singing voice.

Incidentally, my first maneuver was his last; that very same autumn he quit the army and took a civilian job. Some time later I saw him again in, of all places, the streetcar which took me out to Treptow. I bought my ticket and could not believe my eyes when I recognized him as the conductor; but there was no doubt—it was Wittgrewe. He wore a stiff green cap, which looked like a small percussion cap, and a leather pouch over his shoulder; he sold tickets for ten pfennigs, rang a bell every three minutes by pulling a strap, and called out the stops. The sight upset me; I felt distressed, as if a free-roaming animal had been imprisoned in a cage and taught a few pitiful tricks. So this was the splendid Wittgrewe.

Wittgrewe had recognized me too. But he didn't seem pleased—he evidently disliked being reminded of our common past, and to my increasing surprise, he looked upon our riding days as something inferior and insignificant, while regarding his present occupation as a promotion.

Although he didn't seem to attach much importance to it, I visited him at his home. Young people dislike losing sight of persons who have served them as models. And Wittgrewe had certainly been a model cavalryman. The swiftness with which he jumped obstacles, his use of any and all occasions to jump —these presuppose a full-blooded physique and a sanguine temperament. A certain recklessness also has to be taken into account; even Monteron silently tolerated it.

The sight of Wittgrewe's apartment was still more depressing. He lived in the Stralau district—Berlin, "as it cries and laughs." He took me into a room with a heavy buffet of Caucasian walnut, crowned by a crystal bowl. He was married. For the first time in my life I realized that the cocks of the roost have the most unattractive wives. I was particularly surprised that there was not a single engraving or photograph of a horse in the whole apartment, and no sign of the prizes he had won at the contests. Of the old wine-women-and-song atmosphere nothing was left but his membership in the Stralau Glee Club. This was the limit of his social needs.

And on what did he base his hopes for the future? He wanted to become a supervisor, perhaps even an inspector; his wife expected a small legacy, and he himself might some day be elected to the Board of Directors of his club. His scrawny wife sat with us in silence while we drank our light beer, and I left feeling that I had chosen the wrong moment for my visit. Perhaps it would have been better had I invited him to a beer garden or to the races at Hoppegarten; surely somewhere deep-down the memory of the past was still slumbering—he could not have forgotten everything. Perhaps in his dreams, I thought, Wittgrewe mounted his horse again and, singing, galloped across the open plains, until in the evening the high framework of draw wells on the horizon beckoned to him with the promise of bodily comfort and pleasure.

It was when I mentioned the Polyphemus from Sheffield or Manchester that I suddenly remembered Wittgrewe. When he had kowtowed to the new gods, Taras Bulba must have turned in his grave. Soon I was to learn that his case was not isolated. When we had been stationed in one of the Eastern Provinces, only young recruits from the villages joined us, sons of peasants and farmhands, who from childhood were used to dealing with horses. The years in the cavalry were a treat for them. Later, more and more were absorbed by the big cities and ended up like Wittgrewe. They were hired to do piecework, which was beneath a man's dignity. It could have been done just as well by a woman or a child, or even by a part of the machinery at which they worked.

What they had done in their youth, and what for millenniums had been man's vocation, joy, and pleasure—to ride a horse, to plow in the morning the steaming field, to walk behind the oxen, to mow the yellow grain in the blazing summer heat while streams of sweat poured down the tanned body and the women who bound the sheaves could hardly keep in step with the mowers, to rest at noon for a meal in the shade of green trees—all this, praised by the poets since times immemorial, was now past and gone. Joy in labor had disappeared.

How can one explain this trend toward a more colorless and shallow life? Well, the work was easier, if less healthy, and it brought in more money, more leisure, and perhaps more entertainment. A day in the country is long and hard. And yet the fruits of their present life were worthless compared to a single coin of their former life: a rest in the evening and a rural festivity. That they no longer knew the old kind of happiness was obvious from the discontent which spread over their features. Soon dissatisfaction, prevailing over all other moods, became their religion. Where the sirens screamed, it was horrible. And soon there was hardly a corner left where sirens could not be heard.

Everyone had to become resigned to this. If not, if you wanted to persist in an outdated way of life as we horsemen did, the people from Manchester came for you. The old way of life had disappeared. Now the slogan was: Do or die. Wittgrewe had realized this before I did. I am, therefore, far from criticizing him and the others; I myself was forced to take the same turn.

Here was our situation: the men from Manchester had shown us what was what. We had to give up our horses. So we arrived with tanks "to smoke them out"; whereupon they treated us with a new surprise.

I admit that this succession of ever new models becoming obsolete at an ever increasing speed, this cunning question-and-answer game between overbred brains, had fascinated me for a while, especially when I was employed as a tank inspector. You see, the struggle for power had reached a new stage; it was fought with scientific formulas. The weapons vanished in the abyss like fleeting images, like pictures one throws into the fire. New ones were produced in protean succession.

The spectacle *was* fascinating—on this point I agreed with Wittgrewe. When new models were displayed to the masses at the great parades in the Red Square in Moscow or elsewhere, the crowds stood in reverent silence and then broke into jubilant shouts of triumph. What was the meaning of this thunderous roar, when on the ground turtles of steel and serpents of iron rolled past, while in the sky triangles, arrows, and rockets shaped like fish, arranged themselves with lightning rapidity into ever-changing formations? Though the display was continual, in this silence and these shouts something evil, old as time, manifested itself in man, who is an out-smarter and a setter of traps. Invisible, Cain and Tubalcain marched past in the parade of phantoms.

VI

Now I should describe how all this gradually filled me with disgust; but to do so would lead me too far afield. If I have spoken chiefly of the power aspect of the events, I meant to take a short cut. Everywhere hubris is dominant and great danger threatens.

I was now employed as an instructor, without definite rank, at the tank-inspecting station: I was one of the "new men"— a specialist—but my field was one which, though indispensable, is not particularly respected. On the other hand, I had little respect for my employers. Every master has the servant he deserves. The drawbacks of the profession are well known, but the work also has its advantages; among others, one does not immediately have to play the role of an accomplice. One can withdraw behind facts.

In my free time I was mainly occupied with my historical studies. Since my job made it almost impossible to carry books around with me, apart from a small "iron ration," I used to go to libraries and lectures. I also formed a theory. I imagined that we were living during the period before Actium, burdened with the curse of a universal war, and that this period would be followed by another, in which Actiades would be celebrated—a series of great and peaceful centuries. Of course, in *our* lifetime we would only see misery.

As an instructor I had no difficulty with the technical side of the job, and neither did most of my friends. I even felt a certain passion for it. But anyone who has taught knows that this is not the principal point. In order to penetrate the subject matter there must be, in addition, the love of teaching and the love of learning, the give and take between teacher and student, example and imitation. Beyond the technical problem, there is a personal encounter similar to that of a savage training his sons in the use of bow and arrow, or of an animal guiding its young. I am firmly convinced that one of the high orders of the universe is a pedagogical order.

I felt an inner need to associate with young people. Since I lacked Monteron's super-personal authority, I had to rely on my personality alone. In the beginning, my relation with them was comradely; later I intensified it with a fatherly affection. I had been denied a son though I wished for one, and I was excited to learn how these young men would master their lives. They had been born into an atmosphere of insecurity and had never known men with the absolute assurance of a Monteron. I could, therefore, realize better than they the measure of their threatened situation, their loneliness in uncharted seas, their dreadful position on the brink of nothingness.

I do not refer to physical dangers, though these, too, weighed heavily upon my mind on the last evening before we had to separate. The young men were sitting close together, huddled like birds in a nest. Of course, the usual phrases had been uttered: "We'll show them," and the like; but there was also an undertone of anxiety, a dark shadow, impossible to banish. And I thought, seeing them sit before me: "Yes, soon you will leave—for a place where no teacher can follow you. But what will await you there?"

It became more and more unbearable for me to know of their loneliness out there. Two or three times I succeeded in getting permission to accompany them; although this was frowned upon and, indeed, was of scant use, since all too soon the moment comes when we have to abandon those close to us. As if separated from them by an ocean, we cannot bring them aid. I would have been happy to risk my own life for them, since I no longer had much to expect in this world—I had amortized myself. But the bullets passed me by.

Time and again I was amazed at their courage, their capacity for endurance. When the politicians were at their wits' end, these young men had to step in and pay the debts of their fathers and forefathers. Remember: it was no longer a question of cavalry charges; they were sent into miserable furnaces! And they went without a word of reproach. In this respect I believe I saw slightly more than Monteron would have, because the zone of profound, anonymous suffering that begins below the established orders was bound to be hidden from him.

I didn't think much about politics. I had a feeling that like Lorenz we were all jumping out of windows, and sooner or later we were bound to crash. At the moment we were, so to speak, suspended in mid-air. I mentioned before that a number of my friends had advanced into high military and political positions. I stayed modestly in their wake. It was, after all, necessary to join something.

No doubt, there are some insights which are not only useless but rather harmful. He who looks too closely into the kitchen spoils his appetite. That our cause had its seamy side, and that not everything on the opponent's side was as black as it was painted—to know this and to express it was unnecessary for me. My attitude made me suspect both sides and deprived me of the advantages of partisanship.

I was a skeptic, and my chief weakness was that I lacked

the unscrupulousness of the party member—a weakness soon recognized. Very closely connected with this trait was my bias toward the underdog, which frequently caused me to make strange changes of position. Later I shall return to all this when I talk about Spichern Heights.

Such peculiarity and weakness of character did not remain a secret; so in spite of my satisfactory work, I did not get ahead. Charges of sophistry, hairsplitting and indecision accompanied me in all my service records. In any office or organization, there are clever chaps with whom one must be cautious: during the Asturian campaign a chief of staff distinguished himself by writing on my conduct sheet: "Outsider with defeatist inclinations." Since he really expressed it concisely, I shall profit from his mental feat and talk of my defeatism whenever this quality, which complicated my career, has to be mentioned in the future.

It was at this point that my listing changed from party member to specialist—although this corresponded with my inclinations, the identification was nevertheless unfavorable for my prospects. There was an additional obstacle, which I realized only by degrees: the fact that I could be sure of reaching an audience of a hundred or two but not of a thousand or more. This seems strange at first sight, since if one has the ability to make an impression, a quantitative extension of it should be irrelevant. But that is not the case, though it took me many years to find it out.

As matters stood, I could manage well enough with my specialist's knowledge on the one hand and my personal inclination on the other, but all this was not sufficient when I was confronted by more than my two hundred students. Facing larger units, a conclusive judgment on the state of the times is expected in addition to everything else. This judgment needn't be right, but it should be conclusive. Monteron could deliver such judgments; therefore he was the right person to head a military academy. I lacked them—I had the perspective of a man who is jumping out of the window. Too intelligent for the vulgar certainty of a party member, I nevertheless failed to reach any stable valuations of my own. A secret is attached to inner certainty, and one needs too many big words to express it; but it may be described as an armor which protects one, at whatever level of intelligence, against the world. If I may say a word for myself, at least I have never simulated certainty.

As for the chief of staff in Asturia—he reached the same conclusion with less effort when he supplemented my record with the postscript:. "Unsuited for positions of leadership." His name was Lessner; he belonged to the younger generation and made amazing, instantaneous judgments which for some time have been admired, if not idolized, to an increasing degree.

These were the reasons why I accomplished little. I spent those years in ever-changing theaters of action but with consistent inclinations. We ourselves are the last to notice that we are not making any headway. It is brought to our notice from the outside; former students suddenly emerge as our superiors. As we grow older, the respect we receive diminishes: the disproportion between our age and our position becomes evident, first to other people and finally to ourselves. Then it is time to retreat.

Help, if it comes, frequently turns up from an unexpected quarter: from the weak. This happened to me when I met and married Teresa. My defeatism reached a climax: I went the whole distance, finally turning my back on the struggle for power. It all seemed meaningless and futile, a wasted effort, time lost. I wanted to wipe it from my memory. I came to recognize that one single human being, comprehended in his depth, who gives generously from the treasures of his heart, bestows on us more riches than Caesar or Alexander could ever conquer. Here is our kingdom, the best of monarchies, the best republic. Here is our garden, our happiness.

My taste returned to simple, natural things, to the always accessible pleasures. Why was it, then, that the past now returned like a wave that seizes and sucks under the swimmer who has already reached his island? And why did it have to happen in an ugly, discreditable form? Was it a bill presented me for intelligence wasted in the turmoil of the times? Or did I feel so uneasy because my vision had been sharpened?

VII

These were the thoughts that oppressed me while I looked out over the meadowland with the brook running through it. The peasant was still drawing his furrows, and little by little the brown surface of the plowed-up earth increased in extent. His was a better balance sheet than mine.

Thoughts do not assail us in the way I have been reporting them, assembled coherently and all accounted for. We arrange them in a logical juxtaposition which they do not have when they rise in our mind. There they shine like meteors in the firmament—now as places, now as names, now as amorphous signs. The dead mingle with the living, and dreams with actual experiences. What are these portents; where do we wander at night? I saw the noble face of Lorenz who jumped out of the window. Wasn't this our common destiny, our own reality? Some day, we too would bash our heads in.

There had been times when life was almost exclusively concerned with preparation for this moment; perhaps those times had been less senseless than the present.

A slight noise made me start. Someone must have entered the room. Jumping to my feet, I found myself confronted by an old man who was contemplating me. He must have come from his study. Its door stood open, and I could see the corner of a large table, which, in spite of the hour, was still lit by a lamp. The table was covered with papers, written and printed, and with opened books.

The stranger was a little old man—but while I was registering these facts, I felt that they did not mean anything. Was he really a stranger? And was he really old and little? Of a great age, certainly, because I could see his hair shining white under the green visor which shaded his eyes. Moreover, his features revealed a cast that is molded and imparted by a long life. A similar cast can be observed in the faces of great actors who have mirrored the spirit of their times. In them, however, destiny works, as it were, in the hollow mold. It had worked in this man at the core. He was not an impersonator.

Establishing his age was of secondary importance, since spirit is ageless: this old man was more capable of taking risks—whether physical, moral, or spiritual—than a great many young people, and he would come off better, because he combined power and insight, acquired cunning and innate dignity. What was his heraldic beast? A fox, or lion, or one of the large predatory birds? I rather imagined it to be a chimera, like those which roost on our cathedrals and look down on the town with a knowing smile.

In the same way that he seemed to be old and yet not old, he was also small and yet not small; his whole bearing belied the impression of smallness and age. I had often met eminent persons—I think of those involved with the innermost wheels of our machinery of state and who are very close to the invisible axle. Some were men whose names appear in all the newspapers, some were total strangers. Good or evil, active or inactive, they all had something in common, something imposing, which is recognized, if not by everyone, then by a great many people, especially those with simple rather than complicated natures. A philosopher, for instance, a rearranger of facts and ideas, who is endowed with this spirit, can fascinate his listeners even when they don't understand a word of his lecture. Spellbound, they will hang on his lips. The same effect is possible in other fields. Apparently a direct recognition of greatness exists, wholly independent of intellectual comprehension. We react like magnets to an electric current. That his impact is composed of letters, words, texts is another matter—often they even weaken the power of attraction. But although the phenomenon is not easy to describe, since it has no definite form, it translates itself into works and action, into mental and moral symbols. It may even exert its influence through inactivity—perhaps through asceticism, sacrifice, and meditation. In any case our recognition underlies the disclosure and precedes it. A dim feeling corresponds to the undifferentiated impression. It's as though we said to ourselves: "He's got something," or we simply sense a breath of mystery.

And this is what I felt at the sight of Zapparoni. I thought: "That man has the formula" or, "He is an initiate, one of the elect." Suddenly, "knowledge is power" took on a new, immediate, and dangerous meaning.

Above all, his eyes were extremely powerful. They had the royal look, the open gaze, revealing the white of the eyeball above and beneath the iris. The impression was at the same time slightly artificial, as if it resulted from some delicate operation. Moreover the eye had a fixed stare, peculiar to people of southern countries. It was the eye of a big, blue, century-old parrot, with the nictitating membrane twitching over it. This was not the blue of the sky, not the blue of the sea, nor the blue of precious stones—it was a synthetic blue, fabricated in remote places by a master artist who wished to excel nature. Such a bird had flashed on the edge of primeval streams and flown over the clearings. Sometimes a shrill red and a fabulous yellow darted out of its plumage.

The iris of its eye was the color of amber; exposed to the light, it showed a tinge of yellow, while in the shadow, it looked brownish-red with age-old inclusions. This eye had seen enormous copulations in realms where procreative power is not yet sporadic, where land and sea intermix and phallic rocks loom up at the delta. It had remained cold and hard like yellow cornelian, untouched by love. Only when it looked into the shadow did it become dark and velvety. The beak, too, had remained hard and sharp through having cracked nuts, hard as diamonds, for more than a hundred years. Not a single problem remained unsolved. The eye and the problems —they fitted one into the other like lock and key. His look cut like a blade of flexible steel. Then the objects moved back into their accustomed places.

I had always believed that Zapparoni's monopolies rested upon the skillful exploitation of inventors—but one look was sufficient to see there was more at work in him than a mercurial intelligence which derives profit from Plutonian zones. Jupiter, Uranus, and Neptune were in powerful conjunction. It was probably more true that this little old man knew how to invent the inventors—that he found them whenever his mosaic required.

Only later did it strike me that I had immediately known who it was that confronted me. This was remarkable because the great Zapparoni, as every child knew him, did not in the least resemble the person whom I was facing here in the library. Zapparoni films had developed a picture of a benign grandfather or a Santa Claus, with workshops in the snow-covered forests, where he employed gnomes and racked his brains to find out how to amuse all the children, great and small. "Once again and year by year——": on this note the catalogue of the Zapparoni Works was tuned, a book which was looked forward to every October with an eagerness never enjoyed by any fairy tale or utopian novel.

Zapparoni must certainly have had a deputy to play this role, perhaps an actor, perhaps a robot. It was even possible that he employed several such shadows or projections. This is one of mankind's ancient dreams, and has given rise to special turns of phrase: "I cannot be in four places at once," for instance. Evidently Zapparoni not only believed it to be possible, but considered the division a profitable extension and intensification of his personality. Now that we are able to enter apparatuses and leave parts of ourself within them—for instance, our voice and our image—we enjoy certain advantages of the antique slave system without its drawbacks. If anyone understood this, it was Zapparoni, the connoisseur and developer of automatons as objects of play, entertainment, and luxury. One of his likenesses, elevated to an ideal, paraded in the Sunday supplements and on the television screen with a more convincing voice and a more genial appearance than those nature had given him; another gave a lecture in Sydney, while the Master, comfortably meditating, rested in his study.

I was slightly shaken in the presence of this un-likeness which affected me like an optical illusion and made me doubt the man's identity. Was this the right man? But he must be, and the good grandfather was his deputy-director. His voice was pleasant, by the way.

VIII

"Captain Richard," he said, "Mr. Twinnings has recom-
mended you to me, and I value his judgment. He thinks that
you'd like to devote yourself to better, more peaceful things,
just as he has done. Well, it is never too late for that."

As he spoke, he stepped out onto the terrace and motioned
me to a chair. I sat down, dazed: the dentist's first probe
touched the sensitive nerve at its root and at the seat of the in-
flammation. The interview began in the most unpromising
way possible.

In Zapparoni's eyes I was, of course, a doubtful character,
as I undeniably was in my own. That he had gently shown his
lack of respect should not have offended me; indeed, in my
present situation, it was entirely appropriate for me to be
oversensitive.

But with his contemptuous allusion to my former profession he had touched an old unhealed wound. I knew that the
affairs I had been engaged in were, in the eyes of inventors
and builders like Zapparoni, things only one step removed
from the "stealing of horses." One would do well to dissociate
one's self from them, but I could not imitate Twinnings.

A man like Zapparoni could say what he wanted to—it
sounded well. It had authority, not only because he could

buy up the press, which paid homage to him in the editorial
and the advertising departments, but principally because he
was an embodiment of the spirit of the age. This homage had,
therefore, the advantage that it was not only paid for, but that
it was, at the same time, sincerely felt—it demanded nothing
but wholehearted approval from both the intelligentsia and
the moralists of the press.

I must, of course, admit that Zapparoni really could pass for
the showpiece of that elated technical optimism which dominates our leading minds. With him, technology took a new
turn toward downright pleasure—the age-old magicians'
dream of being able to change the world by thought alone
seemed almost to have come true. In addition, there was the
enormous effect, which any head of state could envy, produced by those photographs of him always surrounded by
crowds of children.

Everything devised, constructed, and mass-produced at
Zapparoni's made life much easier. It was not considered good
form to mention that these things were at the same time dangerous, but it was difficult to deny this danger. Although
during the last decades, no major conflagration had occurred,
a series of local crises which had flared up caused the Great
Powers to make a careful estimate of the harm they were confident of bringing about. It was clearly evident then that the
Zapparoni Works played a leading role on this balance sheet
and that, without much alteration, all his lilliputian robots and
luxury automatons could contribute not only to the improve-
ment but also to the shortening of life. The only thing these
Great Powers had in common was the disgusting habit of
mutual spying—the cowardly triumph of calculating brains
over courage to live.

By and large, the Zapparoni Works resembled a temple of
Janus with one bright and one dark portal, and when clouds
were gathering on the horizon, a stream of fiendishly devised,
murderous tools began to pour forth from the dark gate. At

the same time this dark gate was taboo; actually it should not have existed at all. But time and again extremely disquieting rumors leaked out of the construction department, and it was with good reason that the workshop for models was located in the innermost restricted area. The job opening was very likely connected with such matters.

I am certainly far from eager to contribute to that favorite theme: "Why do all the wrong things happen?" Eventually the worst *will* happen. Rather I am concerned with a particular query which often haunted me before and which I was again acutely aware of after Zapparoni's humiliating words of welcome. My query is this: Why are those who have endangered and changed our lives in such terrifying and unpredictable ways not content with unleashing and controlling enormous forces and with enjoying their consequent fame, power, and wealth? Why must they want to be saints as well?

This question had especially bothered me when I was employed as a tank inspector. Among the few books I carried with me at that time (along with Flavius Josephus) was *The Conquest of Mexico* by Prescott. The fascination of this book lies in its evocation of man's rigid taboos and obsessions during a late stone-age civilization where priesthoods and sun temples and human sacrifices abounded. We see, as through a narrow chink, impassive faces seemingly carved of stone, and the streams of blood which flow down through the grooves and drains of the altar in the Great Teocalli. No wonder the Spaniards believed that one of the vast abodes of Satan had opened up before their eyes.

But isn't it possible that, when once again the curtain of the great world stage has fallen, no less horrified eyes may be directed on us and on our saints? We do not know how we shall appear in the history books of future centuries or at the great judgment of the dead on civilizations. Perhaps such a wizened old blood-priest will be preferred to any of our saints.

For instance, our increasing speed, which began at the end of the eighteenth century like the start of a *salto mortale*—how shall it be judged? At a certain point in time we can begin to speak of a dynamite civilization (it is no accident that the highest prize for cultural achievements is provided from a dynamite fund): the world is filled with the noise of explosions—from the rapid, diminutive explosions which set in motion myriads of machines, to the explosions which threaten continents. We walk through a panorama of pictures, which, if we have not fallen under its spell, reminds us of a large lunatic asylum—here we see an automobile race, in the course of which a car drives among the spectators like a missile, mowing some dozens of them down; and there, a "pattern bombing," by which a squadron of bombers rolls up a city like a carpet, in a few minutes dissolving in smoke a work of art which took a thousand years to complete. A luxury airliner crashes to the ground, wrapping itself in red flames. Crew and passengers—men, women, and children—are charred into mummies within the blazing fuselage. Beauty and radiance, jewels, silk, and diamonds evaporate in the blaze.

And such flares illumine our planet daily. After having seen one of them at close range in all its grisly hideousness, I boarded airplanes only reluctantly. At times I was forced to participate in a flight called, in professional jargon, a "flying carrousel"—a circling flight over the training fields for the purpose of observing and discussing the movements of the tanks. I was aware of the risk. But I was not adventuresome enough to put up with this risk in order to save a little time on a pleasure trip. In such a lottery, one is much more likely to draw a blank than the first prize.

We marvel at Mexico and Babylon and overlook the no less astonishing things in our own world. We marvel that a man like Caligula laid claim to divine tribute and overlook how often similar incense is offered in our day. High honors are given to those who discover a formula or contrivance which will shake the foundations of the universe. Perhaps this tendency aims at a *grand prix* that can be no longer conferred by human beings.

That Zapparoni should feel superior to a cavalryman and patronize him was as absurd as a shark passing judgment on its own teeth, which are, after all, its most efficient part. Horsemen have existed for thousands of years, and the world has continued to exist in spite of Genghis Khan and other gentlemen who came and went like the tides. But when saints like Zapparoni began to appear, the earth itself was threatened. The peaceful stillness of the forests, the depth of the ocean, the outermost part of the earth's atmosphere were in danger. Even in peace they had brought about greater evils than any tyrant or warlord had ever imposed; they prepared poisons which no one before had imagined or even known by name. Each day their machines took a toll equal to the casualty list of a single battle, and the yearly toll equaled that of a war—and in what a ghastly manner.

Behind all this was a brutal and ruthless use of intellect which basically recognized only one tendency—that which at the same time shortened, mechanically increased, and accelerated production. But could they create an olive tree or a horse? With all their enormous potentialities they could, of course, build cities, but not the smallest dwelling of the kind once built by a simple mason or a carpenter. Certain naïve souls even commissioned them to build churches, though one would not want even a garden pavilion as a gift from them. The churches they got were built in a style suitable only for pillboxes, airplanes, and refrigerators; there they celebrated their religious rites before a congregation that considered penicillin more effective than any sacrifice of the Mass.

I had admired these super-philistines long enough—these servants of forces unknown to them. As long as such admiration lasts, destruction will increase and human standards decrease. A mind that endangers worlds cannot create a fly.

The huge scaffolding reveals itself as a scaffold indeed. If knowledge is power, one must know first what knowledge really is. That Zapparoni had reflected on this was clear by his look—he was an initiate; he knew. His thoughts went far beyond techniques; I saw it in his eye. Like a chimera, he looked across the gray roofs; he had flashed over the primeval forest in light blue plumage. A glimmer of the immaterial color had splintered off into our times. His scheme and ambitions were bound to aim at something higher than satisfying the ever-increasing hunger of the masses for power and luxury.

His eye had primeval inclusions. Did it recognize the inclusion of timelessness in a new cosmic moment, in the delusion of Maia with its infinite abundance of images that fall back into the basin like drops of water from a fountain? Did his eye look back with nostalgia to the immense forests of the Congo where new races are growing up? Perhaps he would return there after his bold flight into the super-worlds. Black historians would then evolve their theories about him, as we do about the palace of Montezuma.

I should have liked to discuss these questions with him, since we are all haunted by the possibility that there may be some hope for the future. A great physicist is always a metaphysician as well; he has a higher concept of his knowledge and his task. I should have liked to look at Zapparoni's map of operations. These plans would have been more valuable to me than even the fulfilment of the request which had led me to him.

However, far from asking me to join him in his study, the great man received me as a chief Brahmin might, when, in the temple of the goddess Kali, he is asked for alms. He received me with a platitude.

IX

For a moment I had forgotten that I was here as a job applicant, but only for a moment. If anything could have lifted
me out of my misery it would have been a word about our
world and its meaning from the mouth of one of its augurs—
a brief hint from an authority.

Zapparoni had as many faces as his work had meanings.
Where was the Minotaur in this labyrinth? Was he the kind
grandfather who made children, housewives, and small gardeners happy? Was he the contractor who moralized about
the army and, at the same time, equipped it with ingenious
weapons? Was he the daring engineer who was concerned
solely with the play of the intellect and who wanted to describe a curve which led back to basic forms? Or was he simply
trying to devise a new armature such as those observed in all
classes of the animal kingdom, an armature by which nature
harnessed the intellect, drawing upon it as means? It would
explain many a naïve trait, surprising in the protagonists.

Above all—what was his attitude toward man, without
whom all his work was meaningless? It originated in man and
must return to him. A rose or a vine may be conceived without a trellis, but never the other way round. Did he want to
dominate man, to paralyze him, or to lead him into fabulous

realms? Was automation, in his eyes, an enormous experiment, a test to be passed, a question to be answered? I thought him capable of theoretical, even theological reflections; I had seen his library and had looked into his eyes.

It is a great privilege to hear from the mouth of an initiate what struggles we are ensnared in and what the meaning is of the sacrifices we are required to make before veiled images. Even if we should hear something evil, it would still be a blessing to see our task as something beyond a senseless cycle of recurrence.

But it was not for me to question—quite the contrary. Zapparoni's first words had acted on me like a cold douche. For a short moment I was tempted to defend myself. But since this would have been unwise, I contented myself with saying: "It is very kind of Your Excellency to receive me personally."

From Twinnings I gathered he was entitled to this form of address and to many others as well.

"Do call me simply by my name as all the workers in our plant do." He did not say *my* plant or *my* workers. We had settled down in two garden chairs and looked out over the meadows. Zapparoni crossed his legs and regarded me with a smile. Wearing slippers of soft leather, he gave the impression of a man who spends his mornings comfortably within his four walls. But he looked more like an artist, a successful novelist, or a great composer—someone who has been without material worries for a long time and who is sure of his means and his appeal.

The hum of the plant came to us from the distance. I felt that in a moment he was going to ask me questions. I was prepared for them, but had not arranged any answers, as I once used to do for similar interviews. Surely, every applicant wishes to make a special impression, one which represents the ideal picture of himself he carries in his mind. He submits his own advertisement. In this case any such presentation was out of the question simply because I didn't exactly know what was expected of me. Besides, interviewing techniques have made enormous progress in our time. Even though the interviewer scarcely ever finds out what the man *is*, he grasps with great perspicuity what he is *not* and what impression he struggles to give. In such a situation, therefore, it is always best to answer quite extempore.

"You came at just the right moment," he said, "to help me clear up a detail which has struck me in a book I am reading."

He pointed to his study. "I've begun to read the memoirs of Fillmor, whom you probably know—you must have been near-contemporaries at school."

This remark was more apposite than Zapparoni supposed, unless he had meant to provoke me. Fillmor was now one of our high commanders. I knew him well; we had both been in Monteron's class. He had served with the Parchim Dragoons and had been sent by them to the military academy. Like Twinnings he was attracted to Anglo-Saxon manners: both were from Mecklenburg. The Court of this little grand duchy modeled itself on the English pattern, and many who came from there had a London touch.

Fillmor was very much like Lessner, but far superior to him, a typical "First"—even at that time it was taken for granted that a brilliant career was in store for him. Even Monteron, who didn't like him particularly, never questioned that he had a first-class intelligence. In general, Fillmor had no friends; he exuded a frosty atmosphere, in which he himself felt at ease. This distinguished him from warmhearted characters like Lorenz or from bons vivants like Twinnings, whose friendship was coveted. Accordingly, Lorenz was drawn to the troop, Twinnings to the post of staff officer, and Fillmor to a commanding position.

We had started together—he, the man of success; I, the man of failure. It was easy to draw parallels, and I had often drawn them myself. How could his quiet, assured rise be explained—a rise that surmounted catastrophies as if they were

rungs in a ladder? I suppose the main reason was his prodi-
gious memory. He was a pupil who never needed to study
since everything he heard became permanently fixed in his
head—forever imprinted on his memory. If you read a poem
to him slowly, later he could recite it by heart without a single
mistake. No one learned languages more easily: all were
child's play. After he had memorized a thousand words, he began to read foreign books and newspapers, broadening the
range of his historical and political knowledge at the same
time. It was as though he vaulted into the spirit of a language
instead of working his way into it. He showed a similar ability
in mathematics, and even with large numbers, he could solve
arithmetic problems in his head.

All this frequently led to clashes with our instructors when,
for instance, he made an unprepared translation at sight or
when he handed in given problems, having written down
only the problem and the solution. The instructors suspected
him of cheating, until they realized whom they were dealing
with. A long passage from a difficult author, which the instructors had painstakingly chosen in order to torture their
pupils, word by word, for a whole lesson—this Fillmor would
have translated in one minute (had they not curbed him).
Such natures are the terror of schoolmasters. Since they could
not prove him guilty, they tried to change to the *argumentum
ad hominem*. This was also difficult, since Fillmor's conduct
was distinguished by an unobtrusive superiority. Later, on
Monteron's formidable Mondays, no shadow was ever cast on
him. When he had been treated unjustly, he would take his
revenge by waiting patiently for a flagrant error and then reporting it, but only after politely asking permission to speak.
It then became evident that the pedants were less concerned
with knowledge than with showing their own superiority. But
his prank had been well prepared and they began to feel uneasy. In order to ignore his superiority, they had to ignore
him. So the class often presented the spectacle of a "First"

who listened in silence and was never asked a question. The instructors were overjoyed when they got rid of him. But there could be no doubt about his receiving a *summa cum laude*.

His astonishing gift accompanied him in his profession. One is liable to underestimate its advantages, but a good memory for names, for example, is an asset in many fields. We have a direct influence, a personal power, over people whom we know by name, especially in the great world of affairs. Human beings set great value on their names. I was, in this respect, always too definitely guided by my emotions. I knew the names of people I liked or disliked, but forgot those of others or confused them, which is more embarrassing still. Fillmor surprised even people he had never seen before—telephone operators, for instance—by addressing them by their names, thereby giving them the impression that they were his equals.

No one could match his ability to deal with time, space, and facts. His mind must have looked like a control panel. He mastered positions like a blindfolded chessplayer who simultaneously engages in fifty games and is capable of calling up from memory one after another of the chessboards and the position of every single piece. Thus, at any moment, he was informed about military potentialities and reserves, and knew what was possible and which the shortest route to take. He had what is nowadays called "genius," a talent which has universal approval. Moreover, except for an ambition that didn't aim at flashy display, he was almost without passion. He wished only to set forces in motion; he craved only the power of control.

Since Fillmor had no idiosyncrasies and always knew what was possible, he survived effortlessly all the changes in political climate and governments. The waves which beat others down lifted him up. Men like him were always needed by monarchies, republics, and dictatorships of any kind. While I had become a specialist, in order to be only just tolerated, he was the indispensable expert. Those who gain power quickly often remind us of brigands who requisition a locomotive only to discover they can't run it. While they are standing about helplessly, experts like Fillmor arrive and show them how to operate the levers. One sound of the whistle and all the unmoving wheels begin to turn again. On minds like Fillmor's rest the pure continuity, the uninterrupted functioning, of power; without them revolutions would come to nothing, remaining a mixture of crimes and meaningless talk.

It stands to reason that Fillmor's old comrades regarded him as a renegade, while he considered them to be fools. There was probably a good deal of optical illusion in this attitude, since Fillmor stood firm; he remained true to himself as a prototype of the Zeitgeist by which all were moved, but the changes did not touch his integrity. A fixed star of dogged persistence must have influenced him as well. I sometimes thought of Talleyrand or Bernadotte in connection with Fillmor, but he lacked their charm and zest for life. He did not even keep a good table; I know because he sometimes invited his old comrades to dinner, in order to "cultivate the tradition." On these occasions all those who were down on their luck flocked together and let him stuff them with doctored wines and American horrors. This was all he did, and the man who really needed help would have done better to go to Twinnings.

From all this one may conclude that Fillmor was a man without any imagination, since the person who always knows what is possible doesn't occupy himself with the absurd or the impossible—which had been *my* mistake: even as a child I had never been satisfied with the menu of the day; I had always looked for the impossible. All the systems which explain so precisely why the world is as it is and why it can never be otherwise, have always called forth in me the same kind of uneasiness one has when face to face with the regulations displayed under the glaring lights of a prison cell. Even if one had been born in prison and had never seen stars or seas or woods, one would instinctively know of timeless freedom in unlimited space.

My evil star, however, had fated me to be born in times when only the sharply demarcated and precisely calculable were in fashion. There were many days when I had the impression of meeting only prison wardens—wardens, moreover, who voluntarily crowd to these positions, are satisfied with them and enjoy them. "Of course, I am on the Right, on the Left, in the Middle; I descend from the monkey; I believe only what I see; the universe is going to explode at this or that speed"—we hear such remarks after the first words we exchange, from people whom we would not have expected to introduce themselves as idiots. If one is unfortunate enough to meet them again after five years, everything is different except their authoritative and mostly brutal assuredness. Now they wear a different badge in their buttonhole and mention their relationship to another monster; and the universe now shrinks at such a speed that your hair stands on end. In this mountain range of narrow-mindedness, Fillmor was one of the highest peaks.

For a long time, I could also be counted among the admirers of this kind of briskly disposing intelligence. I even admit I had expected much from it, particularly during the years when I was employed as a tank inspector. My attitude may seem that of a man who finds himself coveting a doubtful post because he sees a former comrade in the glare of celebrity. I rest my case. Fillmor had gone from triumph to triumph and had now published his memoirs. Since he calculated everything, this publication was undoubtedly intended to usher in a new phase in his career. In our day, a successful general, a high commander on the winning side, stands the best chance of becoming top dog in industry or politics. This is one of the paradoxes of an age that is unfavorably disposed toward the soldier.

If Zapparoni had spent his morning studying this fellow's memoirs, it was certainly no sheer pastime. What kind of judgment was I meant to pass on this book? The problem was the following——

X

At the very beginning, Zapparoni had been struck by a passage dealing with the start of the era of world wars. Fillmor mentioned the initial great losses, which he attributed partly to the inexperience of the troops and partly to the fact that the enemy had first shown white flags and then, when the soldiers had abandoned precautions and approached without cover, they had opened fire. Zapparoni wanted me to tell him whether I had witnessed similar occurrences and if this was a customary stratagem in war.

His question suited me; I had weighed it in my mind before. Evidently Zapparoni intended, after the unfortunate first words of welcome, to turn the conversation toward a field in which he knew I was on solid ground. This was not a bad start.

White flags? Well, they can be counted among the rumors

which always turn up soon after the opening of hostilities. In part, they are inventions of journalists whose task consists in painting the opposite side black, but there is a grain of truth to them.

In a garrison under attack, the will to resist is not so uniformly distributed as it appears to the attacker. When the situation becomes threatening, cells begin to form—some groups will want to defend their position at any cost, others will regard the cause as lost. Therefore situations can arise in which the attacking troops are alternately lulled into security by signs of surrender and then are fired upon. They suffer the effect, without recognizing the diversity of the impulse, and they confuse juxtaposed with consecutive action. They necessarily conclude that they have been lured into a trap. It's an inevitable optical illusion. Objectively seen, they have engaged in a dangerous affair, without using sufficient caution. It's much the same when we cut ourselves on a double-edged knife and then hurl it in anger against the wall. The person who acts is responsible for the acted-upon—not the other way round. The fault lies with the attacker. The commander who allowed his men to advance imprudently hadn't mastered his business. He had maneuvers in his head.

With an occasional kindly nod, Zapparoni listened to my comments.

"Not bad, even though all too human—and it's good that you find a remedy at once. Heaven protect us against such intrigues. The Field Marshal does not indulge in such circumstantial considerations."

He laughed contentedly and then went on.

"If I have understood you, the situation is somewhat as follows: Let's suppose I am negotiating with a business rival —a firm. I drive these people into a corner—and they make me a favorable offer. I make my arrangements, provide liquid assets, and make reserves available. At the very moment when the agreement is due to be signed, I am notified that I have negotiated with a subsidiary company and that the principal firm has no obligation whatsoever. Meanwhile the market has recovered and they have hawked my offer around. Now the whole deal has to begin all over again."

After a short pause he continued: "This sort of maneuver happens not infrequently. Perhaps I negotiated with partners who overstepped their authority, or maybe they decided to shelve the whole matter in order to worm a better offer out of me later. Or perhaps the agreement was made when all the participants were up to their necks in trouble. Meanwhile the market revives and they try to back out."

He looked at me with a worried expression and shook his head.

"Is it my duty to brood over the things that go on behind the scenes? I was allowed to take for granted that the man with whom I negotiated had authorization to sign. I had losses; I wasted time and incurred expense. Now I have other worries. Who is liable for redress?"

I didn't know what he was driving at; and Zapparoni, in whose voice was an almost threatening note, gave me no time to think about an answer, but began asking me one question after another.

"Whom would you hold liable in my case?"

"In the first place, the firm."

"And if that didn't work?"

"The partner who signed."

"You see, it's quite obvious. One thinks much more clearly when money is at stake. That's one of the good things about money."

He leaned back comfortably in his chair, looking at me with a twinkle in his eyes: "And how many of the fellows did *you* dispose of when you caught them?"

Damn it—it looked as if *I* was the one who had been caught. Memories of past hells woke up in me, memories one would like to forget.

Zapparoni did not wait for my answer. He said: "I should suppose that only a few got off. And rightly so. In these cases everyone is responsible for everyone else, and stakes his life on it."

I had the impression that the conversation was changing more and more into a cross-examination: "Now, if you hold one of the partners accountable—shouldn't those who waved the white flag also have to face the consequences?"

"It seems obvious."

"Do you really mean that? Wouldn't it be more to the point first of all to dispose of those who have been caught red-handed?"

"I must admit that."

"In practice, then, it looks as if in the first heat of anger one neither discriminates nor hesitates."

"Unfortunately you are right."

There was a moment of silence. The sun shone hotly onto the terrace, and only the hum of the bees which pastured on the flowerbeds could be heard. I felt that in this question-and-answer game I was being driven onto a plane whose significance I did not understand. So many pitfalls existed that I was not even able to judge whether I was falling into them. Perhaps the signs were wrong. At last Zapparoni took up the thread again.

"I have faced you with three decisions. You have decided in favor of none, and in each case have given me an indefinite answer."

"I thought you wished to discuss the legal position with me."

"Is it your opinion that every position is a legal position?"

"No, but every position has its legal aspect as well."

"Quite right. But this legality can become unimportant; you'll realize that when you have to deal with contentious people. Besides, any position has both a social and a military aspect, as well as a pure position of weight, and much else.

But enough of this. It would lead too far—to the atomic weights of power and law, to the squaring of the moral circle—it is not our problem. Incidentally—even your theoretical opinion on the case is unsatisfactory."

Zapparoni said all this not sharply but in rather a kind tone. Then he took up in detail the statements I had made at the beginning of our talk. They were absurd, he said; if you put yourself into the totality of the situation, you'd discover that they would benefit your opponent. Did I really mean that the affair, described by Fillmor as a perfidious trick of the enemy, was a question of optical illusion? Wasn't it rather that the attacker was confronted by a number of groups, who acted according to different principles yet without cunning, without malicious connivance? He, Zapparoni, would show me how this might at least be possible.

What if the attack in the open field should fail? Would those groups, who had shown the white flag, insist on surrender? On the contrary, they would be very quick to take up arms again, and a feeling of triumph would run high all along the line. *Here* their unity would become manifest—I am quite certain of it. A defeated force tends to fall apart; a victorious one feels and acts homogeneously. Nobody wants to remain with the vanquished; everyone goes to the victor.

Only in regard to the tactical procedure, the double-edged knife, was Zapparoni willing to agree with me. One must expect anything from one's opponent, he said; it was perfectly obvious that you had to approach him with caution. When Fillmor accused his opponent of treacherous behavior, it was an effective pedagogical simplification, which the troops and the public would immediately understand, while my presentation was academic.

"Did you follow the debate on the Army Bill? They intend to fleece us again of monstrous sums of money for medieval equipment, fit only for boy scouts. Even horses, dogs, and pigeons are listed on the budget. Well, at least the Field Mar-

shal clearly knows why he has to look around for a new occupation."

And so he struck his initial note again. I had not followed
the debate in the Chamber of Deputies. I had not followed
these debates even in my good days. I preferred reading He-
rodotus—or, when I was bored, Vehse's *Court Chronicles.*
In the newspapers I used to skim over the headlines, the news,
and the magazine supplement, sparing myself the rest. Lately,
under the pressure of circumstances, I lacked the time, money
and inclination even for these. At most I studied the want
ads pasted up on billboards. After all, nothing is more dated
than yesterday's newspaper. Besides, I was exclusively occupied with thinking up ways and means of eluding my creditors. This was more important to me than politics.

In any case, I wasn't eager to hear Zapparoni's opinion of
the army. Very likely he thought of it as a department of
his factory, where teams of scientists and engineers worked
in overalls—a company of non-horsemen and vegetarians with
sets of false teeth who loved to press buttons—and where a
half-witted mathematician could cause more damage in a
second than Frederick the Great in his three Silesian cam-
paigns. In those days people like Fillmor had not yet become
field marshals; they would sooner have appointed a half-crazy
man, like Blücher, if his heart was in the right place. The head
still remained a servant. But here, on the terrace, I was worried by more than retrospective glances into the historical
past.

My introduction had not been successful—there could be
no doubt about that. Zapparoni had led me into expressing
my opinions, and then had walked around them like a gar-
dener around a tree, detecting its bare branches. Our session
had resembled a *critique* over some superannuated army
captain, when all the participants of the military board, with
the exception of the captain himself, know from the start
that he will never be promoted to major. Leaving such a ses-

sion, you ask yourself why the whole performance has been put on at all. The joke was that Zapparoni should actually have held my opinion, and I his. Instead of which he had exposed me as a liberal windbag.

Zapparoni rose to his feet; I was sure he would now dismiss me. But to my surprise he granted me a respite. He pointed toward a thatched roof, whose gable emerged out of the foliage at the bottom of the garden.

"I still have a few things to do, Mr. Richard. Perhaps you will wait there for me. You won't be bored. It is a pleasant spot."

He gave me a kindly nod, as if we had finished a stimulating conversation which he was hoping to resume later. I descended the stairs to the garden, surprised and perplexed about the length of time he had given me. Probably it was a whim of his. The interrogation had been a strain and I was exhausted. Glad that it was over, I walked down the path with the feeling we have when, at an examination, we hear the bell announcing recess.

At the first bend of the path I turned around. Zapparoni was still standing on the terrace, looking after me. He waved to me and called: "Beware of the bees!"

XI

In the house and on the terrace a kind of temporal slow motion had prevailed. It was a sensation comparable to that of walking through old clearings in a forest. One might be living in the early nineteenth or even in the eighteenth century. The masonry, the paneling, the textiles, the pictures and books— everything gave evidence of solid craftsmanship. One sensed the old measurements: the foot, the ell, the inch, the rod. One felt that light and fire, bed and board were still managed in the old way; one sensed the luxury of human care.

Although it was pleasant to walk in the soft, golden-yellow sand, out here it was different. After I had taken two or three steps, my footprints vanished. I noticed a small eddy, as if an animal, burrowed in the sand, had shaken itself. Then the path stretched out smoothly as before. But even apart from this, I felt at once that time ran faster here, and that it was necessary to be more on guard. In the good old days one sometimes came upon places which "smelled of powder." Now a threat is more anonymous, more atmospheric; but it can be sensed. One enters "zones."

The road was tempting; it invited dreams. In places the brook ran so close that it formed a border. Yellow iris bloomed at its edge and there was butterbur on the sandy banks. Kingfishers flew so low over the water that their breast-feathers became wet.

The ponds in which the monks had bred carp were overgrown with a green mat, and framed with clear borders. There yellow duckweed floated, and pond mussels and spiral snail shells lay whitening. It smelled of mud, of mint, and of the bark of elder trees—like a damp, muggy swamp. I remembered sultry summer days in my childhood when we used to fish with little nets in similar ponds. We had a hard time pulling our legs out of the sucking marsh, and the same rank smell had risen from our footprints.

Soon I arrived at the boundary wall. The brook continued its course through a grating. At the left a thatched roof emerged, resting on red pillars without connecting walls between and topping an arbor rather than a pavilion. It seemed

designed to give shelter against sun or rain, but not wind and
cold. Part of the roof jutted out like a visor. Under it stood
wicker chairs and a green garden table. Here I was to await
my destiny.

Very rich people love simplicity, and it was easy to see that
my host felt at ease here. Implements, leaning against or
hanging from the pillars, indicated agreeable pastimes: fishing rods, nets, eel baskets, crayfish catchers, tins for bait,
bull's-eye lanterns—in short, the inventory of the inland fisherman who fishes by day and night. Hanging from one of
the pillars was a fowling piece next to a beekeeper's mask; on
another, a golf bag filled with clubs. A pair of field glasses lay
on the table. I could not help being impressed by this idyllic
sight, though I was still aware of a "zone" amidst the array of
still life. Around the pavilion grew a border of tiger lilies.

The field which the peasant had been plowing was now
quite close but empty; he had finished his work. It was high
noon; he had plowed during the classical morning. Bordering
this field was a meadow, so tenderly green that it might have
been imported from Devonshire. A path led to it over a slender bridge. This was undoubtedly the golf course. I took up
the field glasses to examine the lawnlike expanse, clipped short
like velvet. Apart from the holes, not a bare patch or the
smallest weed could be seen.

The glasses, incidentally, were excellent; they sharpened
the sight surprisingly well. I was able to judge because the
testing of optical instruments had been part of my duties during the years when I was with the Panzers. These field glasses,
like opera glasses, were constructed for sighting within a restricted periphery, and they not only brought distant and
semi-distant objects closer, but magnified them at the same
time.

On this side of the brook the meadow continued but was
not yet mown. The grass stood high and was gay with flowers
which, to amuse myself, I brought into my line of vision. The

dandelion already bore its globes of silken down; I could see
each minute hair of the tiny parachutes. Here and there the
ground was boggy with stagnant water. Around these water
holes rushes grew, still bearing last year's spikes. I tested the
precision of the glasses by focusing them on places where the
woolly fibers appeared. It brought the finest fibrils into view.
On the peaty edge of the water hole, a sundew plant, true to
its name, showed tiny dewdrops sparkling in the noonday
light. One of its small leaves had caught a fly, entrapping it
with red tentacles. These were magnificent glasses.

Close behind me, the wall, overgrown with ivy, shut off
my field of vision. It looked as if it would be easy to scale, but
of course, Zapparoni didn't need a wall—or locked iron
gates or ferocious dogs either, since everyone within the
area kept to the permitted roads, as they well might.

The beehives stood within the deep shadows cast by the
wall. Although I had no intention of moving from the spot
where I was sitting in the warm sun, I remembered Zapparoni's warning. Do bees rest at noon? In any case, only a few
were to be seen.

That Zapparoni had cautioned me against the bees, spoke
well for him—it was a kindly remark. Bees are peaceful creatures; one need not be afraid of them, unless one deliberately
provokes them.

There are, to be sure, exceptions. When we were stationed
in East Prussia, a country where riders and horses feel
their ease and where there is a good deal of beekeeping, we
had to be cautious during the time of swarming. Then bees
are irritable and sensitive to various odors: to the smell of
horses sweating after a long ride, for instance, or to men who
have been drinking heavily.

One day we breakfasted in an orchard. It must have been a
festive occasion, perhaps a birthday, since wine and *gold-
wasser* stood on the table. A state of intoxication in the early
morning has its special attraction. We had just come from a

ride and were soon in high spirits. Wittgrewe was also present. The air was delicious, filled with the fragrance of innumerable blossoms. Bees were busily humming back and forth. We soon noted that they were less peaceful than usual and that every so often one of us was stung.

At that age anything can become an occasion for a joke. We'd wait for someone to become King of the Bees: whoever got the greatest number of stings would have to stand treat. Since there was enough to drink on the table, we now sat as motionless as dolls and raised our glasses very slowly to our lips. But the bees continued to attack. Now one of us was stung on the forehead by an insect which had got itself entangled in his hair, now another ran his hand into his collar and a third scored a fiery red ear. We gave up and left, after a stout, red-haired quartermaster, already sweating profusely, had gotten twelve stings and was almost unrecognizable. His head looked like an orange-yellow pumpkin—almost frightening.

"You should never become a beekeeper," the proprietor of the inn told him. Since all the others were stung only once, twice, or not at all, it's reasonable to conclude that bees are selective. I myself was never stung.

Remembering this scene was like hearing an anecdote from the days of our forefathers, and it put me in a gay mood. We were stationed close to the frontier then; on the other side of the boundary a regiment of Cossacks was encamped. Visits and invitations to races or hunts were frequently exchanged. On these occasions horsemen came together in a way we're not likely to see again.

How was it possible that the times darkened so quickly—more quickly than the brief span of a lifetime, of a single generation? It often seems to me that only yesterday we sat together in a beautiful hall, laughing and chatting; then, one crossed a suite of three or four rooms and everything became ghastly. Who would have dreamed when we were carousing with the hetmans that death stood so close behind almost all of us. Though we later fought on apparently different sides, one and the same machine mowed us down. Where are they now, all those young men who, then, had still been trained to fight with lances and sabers, and where are their Arab and Trakehnen horses and the little Cossack ponies from the steppes which so gracefully and yet untiringly carried their masters? Perhaps all this was only a dream.

Zapparoni kept me waiting for some time. My thoughts went back to our talk on the terrace, and my good mood left me. Two questions, three questions—and he had unveiled that side of my character which was important to him! He had led me into my own field, the field where I was competent, and in scarcely a quarter of an hour he had found my weak point, my defeatism—the characteristic which explained why I was not an important man like Fillmor, but a discharged captain without prospects. As for Fillmor, he had never shed a tear over the disappearance of horses. Although, as I remembered, he had cut a good figure on horseback, he had always remained one of those attitudinizing gentlemen we find in paintings by Kobell. The great, the godlike union with the animal he had never experienced.

It takes one a long time to realize one's faults, and some people never recognize them. My fault was that I deviated from the generally accepted codes. In my judgments and, often, even in my actions I differed from those around me; this had been conspicuous in the circle of my family and it continued to be so throughout my life. Even long ago, as a child, I had not liked to eat what was set before me.

We approve of people who have firm convictions, but we do so only partially. Actually, our approval is limited to the manner in which the convictions are expressed. When a great man like Fillmor speaks, he generally expresses platitudes. But he pronounces them with great precision and authority. Hearing him, everyone thinks: "There's something I could have said." In this lies his power.

When the rest of us have a personal opinion about a legend such as the white flags, we'd do better to keep it to ourselves, particularly if strong feelings are involved. Most likely I had roused in Zapparoni a suspicion that, in engaging me, he would only get one more contentious person. Meanwhile Teresa was sitting at home—waiting.

XII

The birds grew silent and I again heard the murmuring sound of the brook in the sultry meadowland. Then I came awake. I had been walking about since early morning with the restlessness of a man running after his daily bread. In such a state, sleep surprises us like a thief.

It must have been a light sleep because the sun had scarcely moved. Sleeping under the midday glare had dazed me and I had trouble in re-orienting myself: the place was unfriendly.

The bees seemed to have finished their siesta; the air was filled with their humming. They were searching for food in the meadow, sweeping in clouds over the foaming flood of whiteness which stood high over the grass, or dipping into its colorful depth. They hung in clusters on the white jasmine which bordered the path; and out of the blossoming maple beside the pavilion their swarming sounded as if it came from the interior of some huge bell which reverberates for a long time after its midday peal. There was no lack of blossoms; it was one of those years when beekeepers say that "the fenceposts give honey."

And yet there was something strange in these peaceful activities. With the exception of horses and wild game, I know few animals, never having found a teacher who inspired me with an enthusiasm for them. It was different with plants, since we had a passionate teacher of botany who frequently took us with him on field trips. How much our full development depends on such early contacts. If I had to list the animals I know, I wouldn't need more than a small slip of paper. As for vermin, whose number is legion, this would be especially true.

In any case, I do know more or less how a bee or a wasp or even a hornet looks. As I sat there, watching the swarms, I sometimes saw creatures flying past which seemed to differ in an odd way from the usual types. I can rely on my eyesight: I have tested it—and not only when hunting game birds. Now, it wasn't difficult for me to follow one of these creatures until it descended upon a flower. Then I saw, with the help of my field glasses, that I had not been deceived.

Although, as I said before, I know only a few insects, I at once had the impression of something undreamed-of, something extremely bizarre—the impression, let us say, of an insect from the moon. A demiurge from a distant realm, who had once heard of bees, might have created it.

I had plenty of time to examine this creature, and similar ones were now arriving from all directions like workmen at the gate of a factory when a siren blows. At first I was struck by the large size of these bees. Although they were not as big as those which Gulliver met in Brobdingnag—he defended himself against them with his little sword—they were considerably larger than a normal bee or even a hornet. They were about the size of a walnut still encased in its green shell. The wings were not movable like the wings of birds or insects, but were arranged around their bodies in a rigid band, and acted as stabilizing and supporting surfaces.

Their large size was less striking than one might think, since they were completely transparent. Indeed, my idea of them was derived mainly from the glitter of their movements as seen in the sunlight. When the creature I now watched hovered before the blossom of a convolvulus whose calyx it tapped with a tongue shaped like a glass probe, it was almost invisible.

This sight fascinated me to such a degree that I forgot time and place. We are gripped by a similar astonishment when we see a machine which reveals a new concept in form and function. Suppose that a person from the early nineteenth century could be transported magically to one of our traffic intersections: for a moment the confusion and hurry would fill him with bewilderment, but after a short interval of perplexity, a certain understanding—some vague notion of the principles involved—would dawn upon him. He would see, for example, the difference between motorcycles, passenger cars, and trucks.

In the same way I grasped the fact that what I saw was not a new species but a new mechanism. Zapparoni, that devilish fellow, had once again trespassed on nature, or rather, had contrived to improve nature's imperfections by shortening and accelerating its working methods. Eagerly I moved my field glasses this way and that to follow his creatures whizzing through space like diamonds projected by strong catapults. I also heard their fine whistling break off abruptly when they came to the blossoms and stopped short. Behind me, however, in front of the hives, which now stood in full sunlight, these sounds gathered into one high continuous whistle. It must have taken subtle deliberation to avoid collisions when the swarms of automatons were massed before they sluiced into the hives.

I must admit that the whole process filled me with pleasure —the kind which technical solutions evoke. At the same time, this pleasure was an acknowledgment between initiates of the triumph of a kindred spirit, for my pleasure was heightened when I noticed that Zapparoni worked with several systems. I distinguished diverse models—almost colonies—of automatons which combed the surrounding fields and shrubs. Creatures of especially strong structure bore a whole set of proboscises which they dipped into umbels and flower clusters. Others were equipped with tentacles that closed around the tufts of the blossoms like delicate pincers, squeezing out the nectar. Still others remained a puzzle to me. In any case, Zapparoni had made this corner a testing ground for brilliant inspirations.

Time passed quickly while I feasted my eyes on this spectacle. Little by little I began to grasp the construction of the system. The beehives were placed in one long row along the wall. Some of them showed the customary shape; others were transparent and apparently made from the same material as the bees. The old hives were inhabited by natural bees, which served perhaps as a measure of the magnitude of Zapparoni's triumph over nature. He had certainly seen to it that calculations were made of the quantity of nectar which one colony of bees gathered per day, hour, and second. Then he had installed this colony next to the automatons.

I had the impression that he had upset these little natural bees with their antediluvian economic system, because I frequently saw one of them approach a blossom which had been previously touched by a competitor of glass and immediately fly away. If, on the other hand, a true bee had sucked first from the calyx, at least a dessert remained. It would seem, then, that Zapparoni's creatures proceeded more economically; that is, they drained the flower more thoroughly. Or, could it be that the vital force of the flowers was exhausted after they had been touched by the glass probe?

In any case, to all appearances here was another of Zapparoni's fantastic inventions. I now saw that the comings and goings near the glass hives betrayed a high degree of methodical planning. It has taken centuries, I believe, to discover the secret of the bees. But I gained a definite notion of Zapparoni's invention after having watched it from my chair for scarcely an hour.

At first glance, the glass hives were distinguished from the old pattern by a larger number of entrances. They resembled less a hive than an automatic telephone exchange. But the entrances were not real; the bees never entered the structure. I could not see where they rested or parked—or had their garage, as it were—certainly they couldn't always be at work. Whatever the situation, the glass bees had nothing to do within the hive.

The entrances functioned rather like the apertures in a slot machine or the holes in a switchboard. The bees, magnetically attracted, inserted their tongues and emptied their glass bellies which were filled with the nectar. After that they were ejected with a force that almost resembled the discharge of a firearm. Given the flying speed, the fact that no collisions occurred during these flights back and forth was a masterly feat. Although scores of units were involved, the whole process was conducted with perfect precision; no doubt, some central control or principle regulated it.

It was evident that the natural procedure had been simplified, cut short, and standardized. For instance, everything that had to do with the production of wax had been eliminated. There were neither small nor large cells or any arrangements related to the differentiation of sexes; indeed, the whole establishment radiated a flawless but entirely unerotic perfection. There were no eggs or cradles for the pupae, and neither drones nor a queen. If one insisted on pursuing an analogy, Zapparoni approved only of sexless workers and had solved this problem brilliantly. Even here he had simplified nature which, as we know, has already attempted a certain economical approach in the "slaughtering" of the drones. From the very beginning he had included in his plan neither males nor females, neither mothers nor nurses.

If I remember the natural process rightly, the nectar which bees suck from the blossoms is worked up in their stomachs where it undergoes various changes. Zapparoni had saved his own creatures this trouble as well, by substituting a centralized chemical process. I saw how the colorless nectar, spurted into the connecting channels, accumulated in a system of glass tubes where it gradually changed color. Having first turned cloudy with a tinge of yellow, it became straw-colored and reached the bottom of the tube in the superb yellow of honey.

The lower half of the hive obviously served as a tank or storeroom which was rapidly filling with the delicious stuff. I could follow the increase on the levels etched on the glass, and during the time that I ranged my field glasses over the shrubs and the meadow, and then refocused them on the beehives, the stores had increased by several degrees.

It is very unlikely that this increase and the work in general was watched by me alone. I distinguished still another type of automaton which flew back and forth alongside the hives or lingered in front of them, as foremen or engineers do in a workshop or at a building site. They contrasted with the other bees by their smoke-gray color.

XIII

Absorbed in the commotion around me, I had completely forgotten that I was waiting for Zapparoni. But he was present as the invisible master. I sensed the power on which this spectacle was based.

When we come under the spell of the deeper domain of techniques, its economic character and even its power aspect fascinates us less than its playful side. Then we realize that we are involved in a play, a dance of the spirit, which cannot be grasped by calculation. What is ultimately left for science is intuition alone—a call of destiny.

This playful feature manifests itself more clearly in small things than in the gigantic works of our world. The crude observer can be impressed only by large quantities—chiefly when they are in motion—and yet there are as many organs in a fly as in a leviathan.

This is what fascinated me in Zapparoni's experiment, and I forgot time and place as a child forgets his school. And although the creatures frequently whizzed past me like projectiles, I also entirely forgot the possibility of danger. The way they radiated from the hives in clusters, threw themselves like a glittering veil over the display of bright flowers, then darted back, stopped short, hovered in a compact swarm—from which, by inaudible calls and invisible signs, the gatherers, one by one, were swiftly summoned to deliver their harvest—all this was a spectacle which both enthralled and mesmerized. It put one's mind to sleep. I cannot say what astonished me more—the ingenious invention of each single unit or the interplay among them. Perhaps it was essentially the dancelike force of the spectacle that delighted me—power concentrated within a superior order.

I should not like to omit mentioning a matter which is characteristic of insights of this kind. After I had closely attended the operation for an hour, I thought I understood, if not the technical secret, at least the system—at which moment I began to criticize and to contemplate improvements. This unrest, this discontent, is peculiar, although characteristic of human nature. Let us assume we come upon, perhaps in Australia, a new animal species we have never seen before; we'd be stupefied, but we wouldn't immediately begin to speculate about improving it. This indicates a different attitude toward creative authority.

A critical attitude, like activity, is one of the fundamental characteristics of our time. Both are interdependent. If the critical attitude should dwindle, there would be more peace and less intelligence, to the benefit of the essential. Neither criticism nor activity, however, can steer the course in such a direction—this means that superior forces are involved.

Today every boy who has been given a motorcycle is capable of technical criticism. As for me, I had been trained in it during the years when I tested tanks. There was always something to criticize, and I was famous in the factories for demanding the impossible. The basic requirements are simple: the tanks must be built with the most favorable potential for attack, mobility, and safety. Each of these factors can be intensified only at the expense of the others. With private vehicles, it is quite different; there cost, safety, and comfort come first. The demands meet only in relation to speed, which belongs to the *principia*. Sacrifices are made to speed, not only in times of war but in times of peace.

As to Zapparoni's setup—after my first stupefaction, the question of expense at once suggested itself. In every respect the glass creatures gave the impression of being luxury automatons. For all I knew, each one of them might have cost as much as a very good automobile or even an airplane. But, like all his other inventions, as soon as they were perfected, Zapparoni would certainly mass-produce them. It was also obvious that from this sort of colony—perhaps from a single glass bee—he could retrieve more honey in one day of spring than from a natural swarm in one year. After all, his bees could probably work as well in rain or in darkness. But how would he be able to cope with the queen bee, the great mother, who gives birth to thousands?

Bees are not just workers in a honey factory. Ignoring their self-sufficiency for a moment, their work—far beyond its tangible utility—plays an important part in the cosmic plan. As messengers of love, their duty is to pollinate, to fertilize the flowers. But Zapparoni's glass collectives, as far as I could see, ruthlessly sucked out the flowers and ravished them. Wherever they crowded out the old colonies, a bad harvest, a failure of crops, and ultimately a desert were bound to follow. After a series of extensive raids, there would no longer be flowers or honey, and the true bees would become extinct in the way of whales and horses. Thus the goose would be killed which laid the golden eggs; the tree felled, from which the apples were plucked.

Granted that honey is a delicious food, an increase in its production is not the business of the automaton industry; it is more a task for chemistry. I thought of laboratories in Provence, in Grasse for instance, where I had seen them extract perfume from millions of blossoms. There, broadly massed, are forests of bitter-orange trees, fields of violets and tuberoses, slopes covered with blue lavender. By similar processes it would be possible to extract honey as well. Meadows could be exploited like coal seams from which not only fuel but countless chemicals are obtained: essences, dyes, all sorts of medicinal drugs, and even textile fibers. I wonder why no one has thought of this.

Zapparoni had, of course, long since carefully considered the question of expense; if he hadn't, he would have been the first multimillionaire to be ignorant of these most astute calculations. A great many people have learned, often to their own detriment, how cleverly rich people count their pennies. They would never have become rich had they been lacking in the talent.

And so one could assume that this experiment had a significance far beyond economics. It might have been the hobby of a nabob who amuses himself after a round of golf or a day of fishing. In a technical age you have technical toys. Even millionaires have ruined themselves with such games, for in these matters no one tightens his purse strings.

The assumption that all this was a hobby was, however, most unlikely, for if Zapparoni wanted to waste time and money for his *menus plaisirs,* his cinema industry offered him enough occasion. Zapparoni films were his big hobby, and he risked experiments there which would have driven anyone else into the poor house. The idea of plays acted by automatons was, of course, an old story; such plays had often been tried in the history of the cinema. But formerly there had never been any doubt about the automaton-character of the figures, and for that reason the experiments had been limited to the field of fairy tales and grotesqueries—with the basic effects of a puppet show or the old magic lantern. Zapparoni's ambition, however, was to re-create the automaton in the old sense, the automaton of Albertus Magnus or of Regiomontanus; he wanted to create artificial people, life-sized figures which looked exactly like human beings. People had taken this idea as a joke, but some had been shocked, declaring it to be in bad taste—the conceit of an immensely wealthy man.

But they had all been mistaken, since even the very first of these plays had an enormous success. It was a luxury puppet show without puppeteers and wires; it was the first perform-ance not only of a new play but of a new genre. The figures, it is true, still differed slightly from the human actors we are used to seeing, but they differed pleasantly: the faces were more brilliant, more flawless; the eyes of a larger cut, like precious stones; the movements slower, more elegant, and in moments of excitement even more violent and sudden than anything in our experience. Even the ugly and abnormal had been transposed into new, amusing, or frightening but always fascinating domains. As presented by Zapparoni, a figure like Caliban, like Shylock, like the Hunchback of Notre Dame could not have been begotten in any bed; even if she had been frightened by something strange and terrible, it could not have been borne by a human woman. And every now and then one came upon the most fantastic creatures: a Goliath, a Tom Thumb, or an angel of the Annunciation through whose transparent body and wings the surrounding objects could be seen.

Thus one might say that these figures did not simply imitate the human form but carried it beyond its possibilities and di-mensions. The voices reached a pitch that put any nightingale to shame, and a depth that outrivaled any bass; the move-ments and expressions indicated that nature had been studied and surpassed. The impression was extraordinary. The public now admired what it had ridiculed only yesterday. (I shall not repeat the praise of enthusiastic critics who saw in this play, performed by marionettes, a new art form presenting ideal types.) One has, of course, to allow for the naïve spirit of the age, which snatched at any daring invention as eagerly as a child at a new doll. The newspapers deplored the fate of a young man who had jumped into the Thames: he had taken

Zapparoni's leading puppet actress for a woman of flesh and blood and could not get over his disappointment. The management, expressing regrets, implied that it might not have been impossible for the fair robot maid to have responded to the young man's courtship. He had acted too impulsively; he had not grasped the ultimate possibilities of technology. At any rate, the success was tremendous and certainly repaid the original expense. Zapparoni had the golden touch.

Anyone who could play with artificial human beings surely had enough entertainment; he need not amuse himself with glass bees. The place where I found myself was no playground, but there are, of course, still other fields where money becomes unimportant. A conversation with a Brazilian came to mind; he once said to me: "It is not yet certain who will gain the upper hand in our country—man or termite."

That these glass bees were collecting honey was, of course, a kind of game, an absurd task for such ingeniously contrived mechanisms. But creatures capable of doing this could be used for almost any purpose, and it would probably be easier for automatons of this sort to collect small grains of gold and diamonds than to extract the nectar from blossoms. But even for the most lucrative business they were still too expensive. Economic absurdities are produced only when power is at stake.

And, indeed, the person who had such colonies at his disposal was a powerful man—more powerful perhaps than a man who commanded the same number of airplanes. David was stronger and more intelligent than Goliath.

On this level economic considerations were entirely unimportant; here one had to enter into another sphere of economy—the titanic. One had to make a different accounting. I couldn't guess the price of such a bee; but supposing it to be a hundred pounds, its cost would seem sheer lunacy to a beekeeper. Other viewpoints are, however, possible: a spaceship, for instance, might cost a million pounds; to both a beekeeper and a Light Cavalryman this was equally absurd. Considering the weird cargo which such a ship was intended to carry, the price was fantastic; yet the cost again became minimal if one considered the damage it was meant to do. Consequently, billions of pounds evaporated into the air without anyone taking into consideration the attack on life and limb. If one could fix only a single little bee to the wings of such a monster and wreck it, the cost of even a thousand pounds would seem only a bagatelle. We must admit that people calculate in our world with great shrewdness, even in the case of machines. Still there are exceptions. Sometimes people are more wasteful, more extravagant even than August the Strong and his minister Brühl, and are none the better for it.

Well, there was no doubt about it—I had come upon a testing ground of the Zapparoni Works, an airfield for testing micro-robots. My suspicion that it was a question of weapons probably hit the mark. We always think first of something of that sort, and of plain utility. But by reducing his bees to workers, Zapparoni had not robbed them of their sting— quite the contrary.

While I was turning all these factors over in my mind, a profusion of more subtle possibilities came into view. What I had been observing was not so much a new medium as a new dimension, opened up by an inventive brain; it was a key which unlocked many rooms. For instance, what if these creatures could be used—as they are used in the world of flowers —as messengers of love between human beings . . . ? But we had better keep to more solid chapters of zoology. And where could a Parliament be found willing to grant even ten pounds for *that* purpose?

XIV

The sight that at first had amused me as a spectacle finally came to delight me as an example of teamwork. But now I began to realize its powerful significance, and like a gold seeker who has entered the land of Ophir, I was intoxicated. Why had the Old Man permitted me to enter this garden?

"Beware of the bees!" How strange that everything he said had a meaning different from the one I assumed. Perhaps he had meant that I should keep a cool head—heaven knows I felt that the spectacle had shaken the hinges of my mind. Very likely the master was testing me. For practical purposes, he wished to see if I could grasp consequences, if I would be equal to his idea. Had Caretti's mind become unsettled in this garden?

"Beware of the bees!"—it might also have been a warning against curiosity. Perhaps he wanted to know how I would behave when confronted with the revealed secret. But up to this moment I hadn't moved from my chair.

My mind was much too occupied to think about my own behavior; I was completely under the spell of the goings on. Back in the old days when an invention was made it was a stroke of luck, and frequently even the inventor himself was unaware of its significance. The models and the gimcrack con-

structions in the museums evoke a smile. But here the consequences of a new idea had not only been understood, but
had been immediately carried out on a large scale and in
detail. A model had been created which exceeded practical
demands, and since its existence pointed to many co-workers
and people who must have known its secret, I understood
Zapparoni's worry about security.

The number of flying objects considerably increased in the
course of the afternoon. Within two or three hours a process
developed such as I had observed during one human lifetime
—the change from the exceptional to the typical. I had experienced this change with automobiles and airplanes. At first
one is amazed at a phenomenon that emerges sporadically;
finally its flashing past is multiplied into legions. Even the
horses no longer turn their heads. The second look is still
more amazing than the first, but we have entered the law of
series—into habit.

Clearly Zapparoni had pushed the development of these
automatons ahead and was manufacturing them in series, as
far as that was possible in his workshops. But it did not look as
if he were preparing a new commodity—one of the surprises which he announced to the public year by year in his
catalogues. Though it might at some later time become a by-
product, here was an entirely independent enterprise; that
much was clear to me when I observed the increased commotion, reminiscent of the time of swarming or the rush hour in
a city. In different formations the moving mass now branched
out into other sections of the park.

Considered as organization, this activity could be inter-
preted in several ways. One could hardly assume the existence
of a central control panel: such a device would not be in the
Zapparoni style because for him the quality of an automaton
depended on its independent action. His international success
rested on the fact that he had made possible in a small area—
his house, his garden—a closed economic project; he had de-

clared war on wires, circuits, pipes, rails, connections. It was a far cry from the hideous aspects of nineteenth-century industrial style.

I imagined instead a system of distributors, of laboratories, accumulators, and filling stations where materials could be delivered or received, as they were here at the beehives, which not only received nectar but obviously delivered power. I saw how the glass creatures were literally shot off, after having emptied themselves.

The air was now filled with a high-pitched, uniform whistling sound, which, if not exactly soporific, at least blurred my perception; it was not unlike the effect produced by hypnosis. I had to make an effort to distinguish between dream and reality in order not to succumb to visions which spun out Zapparoni's theme on their own.

As I said before, I had noticed a variety of models among the glass bees, but for some time now still other apparatuses had emerged in the general swirl, differing greatly among themselves in size, form, and color. They clearly hadn't the slightest connection with bees and beekeeping. I had to accept these new creations as they came—I couldn't keep up with the task of interpretation. Much the same thing happens when we watch aquatic animals from a cliff—we see fish and crabs and even recognize jellyfish; but then creatures rise up out of the depth which set us insoluble and disquieting riddles. I was like a man of a former civilization who stands at a traffic intersection. After the momentary bewilderment he guesses easily enough that the automobiles are a new species of coach. But now and then he will be frightened by structures which seem to him designed in the manner of Callot.

XV

I had, therefore, scarcely penetrated Zapparoni's installation before I thought of improvements. As I said before, this reaction is characteristic of our times. As soon as the opaque figures emerged, I began to become uneasy and puzzled; this, too, is typical of an age when hierarchy is determined by mastery of technical apparatuses and when technics have become destiny. It is a disgrace not to be up-to-date in this field or to be as bewildered as a moron before whose eyes one strikes a match and against whose ear one holds a ticking watch. Such morons, it is true, no longer exist. From childhood on we are trained to make associations.

When I was in school and when I served under Monteron, things were slightly different, although we, too, were drilled in methodical conquest. At that time, however, there was still a preoccupation with what is going on in man. I do not, of course, mean psychology. After the man from Manchester had put me out of action, I knew what really mattered, and I began to make up for what I had neglected. By giving me a fresh incentive, he had taught me to think.

What could they mean, these new apparatuses which now mingled with the swarms of bees? It was always the same: hardly had one grasped a new technical device, when it

created, as it were, its own antithesis. The streams of glass
bees were joined, like opaque beads in a glass necklace, by
multicolored individuals which moved faster as ambulances,
fire engines, and police cars may do in a column of automobiles. Still others circled above the traffic. They must have
been of a much larger size, but I lacked standards of comparison. I was particularly intrigued by the gray apparatuses
that took off from the hives and now closely reconnoitered
the terrain. Among them was one which seemed to be carved
from a dull horny substance or from smoky quartz. It circled the pavilion clumsily, almost touching the tiger lilies and
now and then hovering motionless in the air. When tanks
deploy in a terrain, observers fly above them in a similar
fashion. Here perhaps was a controlling force or a cell trans-
mitting orders. I kept an especially sharp eye on this Smoky
Gray and tried to find out whether changes in the crowd of
swarming automatons corresponded to its movements or followed upon them.

A judgment of the ratio of size was difficult for me since
the objects in question were beyond my experience, and
there was, moreover, no norm in my consciousness. Measure
depends upon previous experience. When I see, no matter at
what distance, a rider, an elephant, or a Volkswagen, I know
their measurements. But here my senses were confused.

In such cases we usually fall back on experience and con-
sult test objects. When, therefore, the Smoky Gray was moving about in my field of vision, I tried, at the same time, to
catch with my eye a familiar object that would provide a
standard by which it could be measured. This was not difficult, since the gray creature had for some time been flying
back and forth between me and the nearest water hole. But
when I slowly moved my head in order not to lose sight of the
quartz thing, I experienced a particularly narcotic effect. As a
result, I could not say whether the changes I thought I noticed on the surface of the automaton were actually taking

place. I saw changes of color as in optical signals, a fading out followed by a sudden blood-red flash. Black excrescences appeared like the horns of a snail.

At the same time, when the Smoky Gray suddenly reversed its motion and hovered for a second over the water hole, I did not forget to estimate its size. Had the swarms of automatons left or did I no longer see them now that my attention was riveted on one point? In any case, it was now completely quiet in the garden and there were no shadows, as in dreams.

"A cut quartz, the size of a duck egg," I concluded, after having compared the Smoky Gray with the spike of a bulrush it almost touched in passing. I knew these rushes well from my childhood; we had called their spikes "chimney-polishers," and used to ruin our clothes in the mud when we tried to pick them. We should have waited till frost had set in, but even then it was dangerous to get to the plant, since the ice around the sedge-lined water was brittle and full of duck holes.

An ideal object for comparison was the fly which adorned a leaf of the sundew plant like a miniature etched in a ruby. This plant, too, was an old friend. On our excursions into the moor we had dug it up and planted it in our terrariums. The botanists list this plant as "carnivorous"—a barbaric exaggeration that has made this graceful little herb famous. When I brought the smoky fellow, which was now flying quite low, back and forth, and almost touching the edge of the water hole, into focus together with the sundew, I saw that, compared to the bees, he was, in fact, of a considerable size.

An exacting, monotonous observation brings on a danger of visions, as everyone knows who has ever pursued a goal in the snow or in the desert, or has driven on endless highways which run straight as though drawn with a ruler. We start dreaming; images get hold of us. . . .

"So the sundew *is*, after all, a carnivorous plant, a cannibal plant."

Why should I have thought that? I imagined seeing the red leaves with their fringes of sticky tentacles enormously enlarged. A keeper threw food to them.

I rubbed my eyes. A vision had deceived me in this garden where the diminutive became large. But at the same moment I heard inside me a shrill signal like that of an alarm clock, like the warning signal of a car approaching with brutal speed. I must have seen something prohibited, something vile.

It was an evil spot. Greatly alarmed, I jumped to my feet for the first time since I had been sitting here and directed my glasses toward the water hole. The Smoky Gray had again come closer; he no longer flew back and forth but circled around me, his feelers quivering. I paid no attention to him. I was fascinated by the sight toward which he had directed me like a pointer to partridges.

The sundew was as tiny as before. A fly should be a hearty meal for it. But close to the plant, lying in the water, was something red, and obscene. I brought it into sharp focus. Now I was wide awake: this was no delusion.

The water hole was encircled by rushes as by a fence, through the gaps of which I saw the muddy, brown puddle. Leaves of aquatic plants formed a mosaic on it. On one of these leaves was the red, obscene object. It stood out in clear relief. I examined it once again; there could be no doubt: it was a human ear.

An error was impossible: a cut-off ear. And it was equally indisputable that I was in my right mind and that my faculties of judgment were undimmed. I hadn't drunk any wine or taken a drug; I hadn't even smoked a cigarette. Partly because of my empty pockets I had lived a very sober life for a long time. And I do not belong to the kind of person, like Caretti, who suddenly see what is not there.

Now I started scouring the water hole methodically and with increasing horror: it was dotted with ears. I distinguished large ears and small, well-shaped and ugly, and all had been severed with neat precision. Some, like the first one I had detected when pursuing the Smoky Gray, were lying on the leaves of the aquatic plants. Others were partly covered by the leaves; still others gleamed upward indistinctly through the brown marsh water. At this sight, like a wanderer who walks along the seashore and suddenly comes upon the abandoned remains of a cannibal fire, I was suddenly seized by nausea. I realized the provocation, the shameless challenge, that was intended here. It led to a lower level of reality. It seemed to me as if the activities of the automatons, which only a short time before had held me completely spellbound, had now ceased; I was no longer aware of them. For all I knew, everything might have been a mirage.

At the same moment a chilling breath touched me—the closeness of danger. My knees suddenly felt weak and I sank back into the chair. Could it be that my predecessor had sat here before he disappeared? Could one of these ears have been his? I felt a burning sting close to my hair. Now there was no longer a job at stake: it was a matter of life and death, and I could call myself lucky indeed if I left this garden safe and sane.

The case had to be thought over carefully.

XVI

The moment has now come when I ought to speak of morality. This is one of my weak points: therefore I shall be brief. My unlucky star had destined me to be born when there was much talk about morality and, at the same time, more murders than in any other period. There is, undoubtedly, some connection between these two phenomena. I sometimes asked myself whether the connection was *a priori*, since these babblers are cannibals from the start—or a connection *a posteriori*, since they inflate themselves with their moralizing to a height which becomes dangerous for others.

However that may be, I was always happy to meet a person who owed his touch of common sense and good manners to his parents and who didn't need big principles. I do not claim more for myself, and I am a man who for an entire lifetime has been moralized at to the right and left—by teachers and superiors, by policemen and journalists, by Jews and Gentiles, by inhabitants of the Alps, of islands, and the plains, by cut-throats and aristocrats—all of whom looked as if butter wouldn't melt in their mouths. I could no longer bear the sight of a white vest. Zapparoni was right: when the going is bad, you hear shouts of triumph all along the line. But he had not allowed for the fact that not only one's enemy triumphs.

All those who have cheerfully fought side by side with you while the going was good, now assume a hostile attitude. They present themselves in white vests. And you stand in the midst of them like a person shipwrecked among penguins. The unlucky star is in the zenith. This experience belongs to the navigation of the new world.

Actually, the enthusiasm I had felt when I gained an insight into Zapparoni's garden should have made me suspicious: it did not bode well. I had been off guard, in spite of my experiences. But who doesn't have these experiences?

The brutal exhibition of the severed ears had shocked me. But it was inevitable as motif. Wasn't it necessarily the result of a perfection of technique to whose initial intoxication it had put an end? Had there been at any period in the history of the world as many mutilated bodies, as many severed limbs as in ours? Mankind has waged wars since the world began, but I can't remember one single example in the entire *Iliad* where the loss of an arm or a leg is reported. Mythology reserved dismemberment for the subhuman, for monsters like Tantalus or Procrustes.

You need only stand in front of beggars collected outside a railroad station to see that in our midst other rules prevail. We have made progress since Larrey, that surgeon of the Napoleonic Wars—and not only in surgery. It's an optical illusion to attribute these injuries to accident. Actually, accidents are the result of injuries that took place long ago in the embryo of our world; and the increase in amputations is one of the indications of the triumph of a dissecting mentality. The loss occurred before it was visibly taken into account. The shot was fired long ago; and when it later appears in the guise of scientific progress—though it be on the moon—a hole is inevitable.

Human perfection and technical perfection are incompatible. If we strive for one, we must sacrifice the other:

there is, in any case, a parting of the ways. Whoever realizes this will do cleaner work one way or the other.

Technical perfection strives toward the calculable, human perfection toward the incalculable. Perfect mechanisms—around which, therefore, stands an uncanny but fascinating halo of brilliance—evoke both fear and a Titanic pride which will be humbled not by insight but only by catastrophe.

The fear and enthusiasm we experience at the sight of perfect mechanisms are in exact contrast to the happiness we feel at the sight of a perfect work of art. We sense an attack on our integrity, on our wholeness. That arms and legs are lost or harmed is not yet the greatest danger.

XVII

I have said this much in order to indicate that this sequence of pictures and moods in Zapparoni's garden was more significant than it had seemed to me in my first consternation. The intoxication with which I had witnessed the gradual unfolding of Zapparoni's technical ingenuity was followed by a headache, a hangover, and then by the sight of the cruel mutilations. One provokes the other.

Zapparoni could not, of course, have intended to convey this realization to me. He had other plans. Nonetheless, any fresh turn in the struggle for power conceals a lesson which leads far beyond the intention of either partner—it indicates a higher interest.

Beyond any doubt, Zapparoni had meant to frighten me. In this he had been highly successful, and I was certain that, in his study, he was enjoying his triumph: I had walked into his trap. Very likely he was sitting there comfortably with his books, now and then following the messages of the Smoky Gray on his television screen. He would see how I reacted. Fortunately I had not talked to myself. I had enough experience for that. But I had been stupid to jump up.

Formerly, my first—and also best—reaction in a similar case would have been to report what I had seen. Anyone who made such a horrid discovery while walking in the woods would have done the same: you called the nearest police station.

This I ruled out at once. The years when I showed a taste for such bravura were past. To report Zapparoni to the police amounted to accusing Pontius to Pilate, and it was as plain as daylight that it was I, accused of cutting off ears, who would disappear this very evening behind bolts and bars. It would be a fat morsel for the night editions. No—only a person who had slept away thirty years of civil war could advise me to act thus. Words had changed their meaning; even police were no longer police.

Incidentally, to come back to the wanderer—even today he would report finding a single ear. But what would he do when he came to a part of the forest where a profusion of ears were lying around like poisonous mushrooms? You can be sure he would sneak away. And perhaps neither his best friend nor his wife would hear about his discovery. In such a situation we are cautious.

"Leave well enough alone"—this was the principle I had to follow. True, it exposed me to another danger. I would have ignored a crime and neglected my first duty to my neighbor. From there to inhumanity is only one step.

In any case, my situation was critical, whether I met it by action or inaction. The best thing would be to follow the advice I had once heard in a café in Vienna: "Don't even begin to ignore". . . This was the dictate of prudence.

Even then unpleasant prospects remained. Zapparoni might be unsuccessful or go bankrupt. He would not be the first superman to disappear in this fashion. What I had seen in his garden resembled a rehearsal for total mobilization more than an exhibition of models by an international firm. As such, it might come to a bad end, and if that happened a storm of indignation would break loose; and the indignation of those who today sat in a safe corner would outdo those who had fawned on the powerful Zapparoni. The first would wish to compensate, the others to vindicate themselves. But all these penguins would be unanimous in their view of the depraved Cavalry captain who was involved in the scandal of the cut-off ears. "Nothing seen, nothing heard—the classical case," said the chairman, and the heads of the jurors nodded over their white vests.

Since my evil star inevitably guided me toward the defeated, I had been taught a similar lesson more than once—even by people who, for years—even on the eve of the defeat—had been guests at my table. Now in the white vests of lackeys they served the victors at the festive banquet held in their destroyed ancestral home.

As for me, I preferred to continue wearing my old vest; I was used to it and had become fond of it, although it had been damaged on long marches and on hot days when sparks leaped from our tin hats. The vest showed traces of the mud of the trenches, the dust of the barricades, and there were holes in it as well. These went deeper than the vest and deeper than the skin. Even though is was not a white vest, it was a good, trusty garment; it had survived monarchies and republics. I wished to be buried in this vest, and they could save their comments.

I always liked to imagine my funeral—another of my weaknesses. I would die poor and inglorious, but I supposed two or three cavalrymen would stand by my grave with Teresa. In the evening they would have a glass of wine. Tommy Gilbert would probably get drunk again. Since only a few drops were sufficient to make him drunk, I used to wonder why he never had any money. The solution of this riddle was that actually he was always slightly tipsy. It was his normal condition. Even in East Prussia he used to have a tumbler of brandy with his breakfast, before we left for the ice-cold riding academy, lit up by smoke-stained lanterns, where the breath of the men and the horses looked like exhalations from silver trumpets. The smallest amount of alcohol was sufficient to make Tommy sentimental. He was then a source of high amusement. Since he knew me well, he would tell about the things we had done together, not only because he loved to tell anecdotes, but also to cheer up Teresa a little; and, indeed, a smile would lighten her face like a ray of sunshine after a cloudy day. I preferred this to the sermon of a clergyman. I had never allowed Teresa to wear dark clothes. It would certainly be a delightful day.

XVIII

For the time being I was still far removed from such a pleasant end. I was in a situation where one can only make mistakes. The only question now was to figure out which was the least important one and to get my head somehow out of the noose, so that I could return to Teresa. I could not leave her alone. It was a good thing that I hadn't moved from the spot. Jumping to my feet did not, after all, imply much; I might have done it because of the gray thing. I turned my glance away from the water hole and buried my head in my hand, as if I were tired.

The most important thing now was to get out of the park safe and sound, as Caretti had evidently not been able to do. They might cut off as many ears as they liked; moral scruples were not going to trouble me. My head was swimming not because of them but because of a physical nausea which contracted my diaphragm.

I tried to overcome this feeling which I had known since I was a child. Lying below the moral sphere, it did not deserve any praise, just as aversion to a certain food is nothing to be proud of. Some people are allergic to strawberries or lobster or any red foods and cannot even look at them. Others, like myself, for instance, cannot bear to see cut-off ears.

On the other hand, at least in my better days, I never had the least objection to violence. But I preferred it to take place between relative equals; there had to be parity. If, for example, an ear had been lost in a saber fight, it would have certainly affected me as unpleasant but not—as in this case—as revolting. There are nuances, now hardly distinguishable, but nuances frequently make all the difference.

With the absence of equality, the repulsive element gained ground, and this lack of balance produced a sensation of seasickness. The opponent has to be armed or he is no longer an opponent. I loved hunting and avoided slaughterhouses. Fishing was my passion. I became disgusted with it when I heard that brooks and ponds can be fished out by electricity down to the last stickleback. The plain fact, even mere hearsay, was enough for me: from that moment I never again touched a fishing rod. A cold shadow had fallen on the swirling trout streams and backwaters, where moss-grown carp and catfish dream, and had robbed them of their charm. One of our mathematical idiots had been at work again, characteristically confusing fight and murder. Undoubtedly he had been presented with a very high official decoration for it.

When I saw several thugs attack a lone man, or a larger man a small one, or even when a mastiff attacked a toy Pomeranian, not virtue but plain disgust upset my insides. This early variety of defeatism later became an obsolete trait—damaging to me in today's world. I often blamed myself for it, telling myself that, after all, when one has dismounted the horse and climbed into a tank, one's mental attitude should change as well. But these matters are difficult to overcome rationally.

When in Rome, do as the Romans, otherwise you'll have a hard time. This piece of wisdom was taught me first by Atje Hanebut, and with a vengeance. Since this first experience clearly revealed the plain malice of my evil star, it will be mentioned here as an example of all subsequent experiences.

When we think back to all the people who have taught us lessons, we come upon one person who led us from childhood into adolescence. For me and other neighborhood boys this person was Atje Hanebut. At that time he was about sixteen or seventeen, and he ruled absolutely over a gang of twelve-year-olds. He instilled in us a new concept of authority—the admiration for a leader whom one obeys blindly. Such a leader occupies not only our thoughts and ambitions by day, but our dreams by night. This domination, reaching into the world of our dreams, is an unmistakable symptom. As soon as one begins to dream of someone—whether pleasantly or in a nightmare—one becomes a captive. One is even expected to dream of a good author: then he begins to become a force.

We lived on the outskirts of the city, on Wine Street where each house was surrounded by a large garden. At the end of the street was a meadow which every year was flooded for ice skating. When winter set in early, many parts of the meadow were left unmown, and then I could see flowers, a frozen-summer, through the icy surface. My mother complained about these inundations because they drove numerous mice into our home every autumn.

Behind Forrester's Pond, the meadow led into the Uhlenhorst Moor, which was bordered, along one whole side, by a colony of small gardeners; these colonists we called "Cossacks." Our nearest neighbor was Doctor Meding, an eminent physician of the old school, who lived in the grand style. He employed a cook and a coachman as well as the regular domestics. In his consulting room stood a high mahogany desk, on the leaf of which prescriptions used to lie, weighted down by gold coins. He treated poor patients for nothing.

We were allowed to play in his large, much neglected garden. The chief attraction was, of course, his horses. We knew every corner of the stable, the coachhouse, and the hayloft; and we were also quite at home in the living-quarters of the coachman. We were lucky to be friends of Wilhelm Bindseil, the son of the coachman.

In the Bindseil family, horses had played an important rôle since time immemorial. Old Bindseil had served with the dragoons in Tilsit; he could still be seen with a dashing mustache in the photograph of his squadron which hung in the living room. Their motto: "The Dragoons of Lithuania spare no one and do not wish to be spared" was inscribed beneath the picture. To look at old Bindseil, the motto was hard to believe. His talk was rather confused; and the only thing he didn't spare was the bottle of schnapps.

His brother, Wilhelm's uncle, was janitor at the Riding Academy. He wore the Iron Cross, First Class, and had taken part in the cavalry charge at Mars-la-Tour. Wilhelm sometimes took us to visit him, and we admired the great man from a respectful distance. My father approved of this, since he gave us presents of books, which stimulated us in a military direction. We read *The Life of a German Rider, Memoirs of a Lützow Rifleman, The Great King and his Recruit.*

By that time we had already extended our roving expeditions as far as the moor. But these forages were always bound up with risks, and after the business at the barn, we limited our play to the gardens. We had built a little fire on a bank of the moor. Hermann, my younger brother, began to fool around with some smoldering sticks. All of a sudden we saw a dry cluster of reeds flare up. At once, the heather caught fire. First we tried to beat it with branches, but it ate itself into the moor which was dry as tinder; then, when we were already exhausted from our attempts to extinguish the fire and faint from the heat, and the soles of our shoes were red-hot, then the flames began to lick at the barn.

We dropped the branches and ran toward the city as if the devil were after us. But even there we did not calm down:

our guilty conscience drove us on. Eventually we consulted our savings and climbed the Gothic tower of our local church, which was a hundred meters high. The fee for going up was ten pfennigs. For this price we had a bird's-eye view of the grim spectacle of the burning moor and of the three fire brigades that had rushed out to extinguish it. Our knees were shaking from the climb up the countless rickety stairs, and when we heard from far away the tooting of the firehorns and saw the sky all aglow, we almost collapsed. Trembling, we climbed down, crept through the streets of the old part of the town and into our beds. Fortunately no one suspected us. But for a long time afterwards, tortured by dreams of a fire, I would wake up at night screaming; my parents called the Doctor, our neighbor, who eased their anxiety and prescribed an infusion of valerian. In his opinion it was a symptom of puberty.

All this happened when I was still a child. A few months later, when Atje Hanebut had established his reign over us, he would probably have turned the incident into an heroic deed. He set great value on resourcefulness, on not leaving any tracks behind you, and he gave us tasks where we had to prove ourselves. For instance, soon after we became acquainted, he learned that Clamor Boddsiek, son of another neighbor, had stolen a *taler* from his parents, which he was suspected of having hidden somewhere, so that some time might elapse before he spent it. Atje ordered us to search for it. To-day I am still surprised that we found out Clamor's hiding place. By subtle combinations, which would have done credit to a clairvoyant, we divided the area of his movements into squares which we then scoured. He had concealed the coin in one of the flowerpots in his parents' front garden. We took it out and delivered it to Atje. This may indicate the degree of our eagerness to curry favor with him. Viewed from the moral angle, this was, of course, worse than the whole conflagration in the moor; but when we saw Boddsiek for days afterward still vainly digging into the flowerpots, we were only proud of our scouting shrewdness.

There were frequent changes of coachmen at Dr. Meding's —the service was exacting. They often had to wait for him a long time in the open air, while he visited his patients; and particularly in winter, they would help themselves to their bottles, until their master had enough of it. Then they stepped down from their high positions as coachmen to become plain cabmen, who waited in lacquered top hats for travelers in front of the railroad station. This was the reason why old Hanebut had taken the place of Wilhelm Bindseil's father. Old Hanebut, too, stayed hardly a year, since the Doctor lost his temper when he noticed that his horses were losing flesh. He did not take too seriously that his coachmen were boozers, but the animals should have what was due them.

Mother Hanebut was a woebegone woman who waited upon the Doctor. Father Hanebut scarcely enforced any discipline in his family. Either he drove the Doctor on his rounds or was occupied in the stable; the rest of his time he spent in the pub. Sometimes when the Doctor was called in an emergency, he sent for him there.

The son was his own master. He took small, occasional jobs, delivered magazines for the booksellers and books for the lending libraries. In the fall he accompanied the peasants, who arrived in the city with their carts full of peat or cried "White sand" in the streets. The youngsters who tried to ingratiate themselves with him were high school students of a different social class. This did not prevent him from treating them tyrannically.

My father, who had approved of our friendship with Wilhelm Bindseil, was not too pleased about the new connection. Once I heard him say to my mother in the next room: "This new coachman's son is bad company—he teaches the boys real proletarian manners."

He probably meant the jackboots which Atje wore and for which we had pestered our mothers so long that they finally bought them for us; for we imitated him in everything. In these boots one could walk through thick and thin, through swamp and underbrush: they were indispensable for "pathfinders."

This word, which Atje had brought into use among us, was used by him to mean red pathfinders rather than white. When he saw us running to the Riding Academy, he made no bones about his dislike of soldiers.

"*They* have to stand at attention. A pathfinder does not, except at the stake."

He would also say: "Soldiers have to lie down. A pathfinder lies down only when he wants to stalk someone, and not by command—a pathfinder never accepts any commands at all."

And so we were introduced to the jungle. Soon after, some Indians were exhibited at the shooting match of a country fair. They were introduced, in front of a tent, by a barker who called each one by his name and praised him chiefly for the number of scalps he had taken. Sounding as if he had a hot potato in his mouth, the barker cried: "Black Mustang, little chief—a very bright fellow who has taken the scalp of seven white men."

The warriors, who presented themselves impassively to the gaze of the public, were decorated with war paint and wore feathered headbands. Atje Hanebut had taken us there. It was certainly different from the Riding Academy and Uncle Bindseil—the more so, since the Indians held their own on horseback as well. One of our favorite topics was whether or not they could cope on horseback with the Mexicans and other white men. We were convinced they could, and these long talks served the purpose of confirming their superiority against any possible objection. Another result was that we began to read different books.

After supper we used to gather in the loft above the stable, where the harness hung. We sat on the trestles, or on a pile of horse blankets which was Atje's bed, and he read to us *Son of the Bear Hunter.* What a book! High up there it smelled of horses, hay, and leather, and in winter the iron stove glowed, for the Doctor had plenty of wood. Atje sat with the book near the stable lantern; we listened to him all agog. A door opened into a new world. Dressed only in shorts and our jackboots, we crouched half-naked in the overheated loft; now and then, to make us tough, Atje made us run around the ice-cold park.

In summer we were again on the moor. We knew every corner, every peat bog, every ditch. We also could build a fire which did not smoke. On sultry days we lay in wait to catch the poisonous adders which were one of our chief's sources of income. The Mayor of Uhlenhorst paid three pfennigs per head. Atje Hanebut combined this hunt with testing our courage.

The adders came out at certain times and lay on the banks of the moor, either stretched out or in a coil. It took an experienced eye to see them. At first we caught them by holding them down with a forked willow twig and killing them by blows with a switch. Then we learned how to grab them behind their heads and to hold them, still alive, until Atje let them slide into a bag. These were specimens for the terrarium; they were worth more. Finally we had to pick up the swift-moving reptile by its tail and lift it high with outstretched arm. This was a safe grip; the adder, hanging free, could raise itself only a third of its length. In this position it was submitted to the expert judgment of Atje. If it was a specimen for a terrarium, that is, if it was distinguished by its large size or its coloring, it went into the bag; otherwise it was hurled to the ground and massacred. There were pure black specimens, the "hell-adders," whose zigzag band blended with their ground color. They were particularly in demand by snake fanciers.

Anyone who had taken part in these excursions into the moor for some time and was thought worthy by Atje Hane-but, was allowed to enter the great test of courage. Atje knew what is common knowledge among snake catchers: that a snake which is lowered on the supporting hand, settles on it as on any other surface, provided one doesn't move one's hand. The reptile does not regard the hand as a hostile object.

Atje then selected the most skillful of us, and the test became a question of picking up an adder, pointed out by the Chief, and lowering it slowly with one's right hand to the palm of the left, on which the adder was supposed to nestle. It was a miracle that no one was ever bitten; but, as I said, Atje did not allow just anyone to take the test. He knew what he could impose on a person.

As for me, I remember these as some of the most disagreeable moments in a life full of such moments; I disliked these creatures from the bottom of my heart, and they appeared in my dreams as nightmares. A sensation of annihilation ran through me like a blade when I felt the cool, triangular head on my hand. But I stood as motionless as a statue, so great was my desire to please my Chief, to catch his smile, to distinguish myself in his eyes. Having passed this test, we were then allowed to call him by his war name, which we pledged never to betray to others; we also received names and joined his inner circle. Already as a boy he had known how to get a hold on others.

From the past Atje had inherited a quarrel with the Cossacks. This had existed for generations, perhaps even from prehistoric times when different tribes had settled on both shores of the swamp. But Atje, although he was really much better suited to the other side, made himself *our* leader. Over there was a jumble of miserable huts, sheds, gardens, and small pubs into which we, as high school students, couldn't intrude without causing brawls. Because of our red caps they called us stupid bullfinches. No one from either faction would have dared to enter the territory of the enemy alone. The clashes took place mostly during the skating season or sometimes in early autumn when we flew kites.

When Atje Hanebut joined us in our feuds, he introduced some improvements, among which were scouting duty as "pathfinders" and a new weapon, the slingshot—a V-shaped twig equipped with a rubber band. For shot we used marbles or pellets of lead. And as always happens with such improvements, slingshots soon turned up in the camp of the Cossacks, who simply shot with pebbles. All this led to never-ending skirmishes.

Brawls of this kind are usually crowned by excess and also terminate with it when neutral powers intervene. Here it was the same. One morning, rumor spread that a third-grade student—of all people Clamor Boddsiek, the boy of the taler story—had lost an eye because of a slingshot. It turned out later that the injury was less serious than was first believed, but on that first day feeling ran high.

Immediately after lunch we gathered at Atje Hanebut's place; he at once ordered a punitive expedition. It was my mother's birthday, and we were going to have a big coffee-party; my parents had also bought me a new suit. But after I had swallowed my last mouthful, I slipped, like all the other boys, into my jackboots, without changing my clothes, and put the slingshot in my pocket. The business of the eye occupied my whole mind. There was no room for other things.

After we were all assembled, we left the Doctor's garden through the defective hedge, following Atje in Indian file. It was a hot day and we were boiling with rage, Atje perhaps the least of all.

Bordering the Doctor's property, on the meadow side, was the garden of a *Privatdocent*. On very warm days, he used to study in his conservatory, which jutted out into the garden, its two doors always wide open. Since we were in a great hurry and since a straight line is the shortest, Atje Hanebut burst into the study. The horrified scholar jumped to his feet to save his papers which were flying about, and before he realized what had happened, Atje had stormed out through the other door, a dozen boys in jackboots rushing after him. Then we broke through the bordering hedge, and crossed the large meadow to invade the Cossack territory.

The paths between the hedges and fences lay bright in the midday light. We were now in the forbidden domain. Our band had split. With three or four others I ran along behind Atje Hanebut. At a bend in the road, we saw a Cossack coming toward us. He was alone, a schoolboy, with a knapsack slung over his shoulder. Most likely he had been kept in after class; if so, it was an unlucky day for him.

As soon as he recognized us, he turned around and, quick as a weasel, ran back the same way. We rushed after him. He could certainly have escaped had not another bunch of our gang burst out from a side path, barring his passage. He was rounded up. One boy got hold of him by his knapsack, the others arrived from both sides, and blows fell as thick as hail. Our wrath was tremendous.

At first I thought it was quite right that he should suffer— and with a vengeance—for Clamor Boddsiek's eye. A slightly built boy, who hardly defended himself, he first lost his knapsack and then his cap. His nose also began bleeding, though not violently. Incidentally, it was not I who first noticed it, but a boy who hadn't passed the test of courage and who didn't care either; he had joined us rather by accident. His name was Weigand; he wore glasses and, strictly speaking, didn't belong with us. It was this Weigand who first noticed the blood; I heard him call: "But he's already bleeding."

Now I saw it too, and the whole scene disgusted me: the forces were distributed too unequally. I saw our Chief lifting his arm for another blow; the Cossack was now standing with his back against a garden fence. He really had 'had enough. I hung onto Atje's arm and kept repeating: "But he's already bleeding."

It wasn't insubordination that moved me. I simply thought that Atje hadn't yet noticed that the Cossack was bleeding, and I wanted to point the fact out to him. I seized his arm and said those words not in order to stop him, but only to call his attention to an oversight. Weigand had been the first to notice the mistake, and I only passed his news on to the Chief. I was convinced it really *was* only a mistake; there couldn't be two minds about it. Atje would immediately correct it.

In this belief, however, I was completely wrong. Atje shook me off and looked at me with utter stupefaction. Obviously for him not only wasn't it wrong but it was absolutely right that the Cossack was bleeding. Now he lifted his arm again and struck me in the face. At the same time I heard him shout "beat him," and all the others pounced upon me. They were my best friends and they had known me much longer than they had Hanebut. But one word from him was sufficient for them to treat me like an enemy. Only Weigand stayed in the background. But he didn't take my side; he just slipped away. I paid for his liberality.

My horror was so great that, although I realized blows were showering upon me, I actually didn't feel them. My new suit was treated roughly as well. But the torn garment belonged in the picture.

While the others were busy with me, the Cossack had snatched up his cap and knapsack and had scurried away. At last they left me alone and marched off. I remained, leaning against the fence, my heart beating in my throat. The sun glared down on the bushes, but I had the impression that its rays blackened the green foliage. In my mouth was a bitter taste.

After I had stood by the fence for a long while, recovering my breath, I pulled myself together and walked in the direction of the city. Because I had never been there before, it took me some time to find my way out of the tangle of gardens. But at last I came to the road.

Confused as I was, I thought I heard them coming back. I heard the tramp-tramp of nailed boots and hurried shouts.

"There he is—a bullfinch; that's him, he did it." And before I fully realized what had happened, the Cossacks, roused by our invasion, suddenly fell upon me. In no time they had seized me. I heard a big fellow, their leader, shout: "You pigs, the whole gang of you attacking a sick boy—we're going to cure you of that."

This time I felt the blows, and the kicks too, as I lay on the ground. The only luck I had, if you can call it that, was that they blocked each other's movements in their zeal.

On occasions like this, it is amazing how sharply we observe details. I saw, for instance, that in the scramble, one boy was never able to get at me. Again and again he was pushed back; once I saw his face quite clearly between the legs of the others. It was the boy whose nose had been bleeding; I recognized him. Several times he tried to jab me with a slate-pencil, which he had taken out of his schoolbag, but his arm was not long enough to reach me.

Since they were firmly convinced of their right, I would undoubtedly have come to a bad end in this affair. I even heard others come running toward us with dogs. But fortunately, a cart loaded with beer barrels approached on the main road, and two drivers in leather aprons leisurely climbed down from their seat. They flourished their whip among the crowd, taking alternate turns. They established order and had great fun doing it. I, too, was painfully hit over the ear. The crowd scattered in a hurry, and I staggered home more dead than alive.

As I crept through the hall and to the stairs, my father came out of the living room. The birthday party had been over for some time. I faced him in my outfit, of which nothing was intact but the jackboots, with tousled hair and a dirty, unrecognizable face. He assumed that on this festive day I had again been in a scuffle with the gang led by the coachman's son, and this was, of course, an entirely accurate conclusion. I had not only spoiled my mother's birthday but had also ruined, on the very first day, my expensive suit, which had pleased him so much at noon. Moreover, the scholar already had made complaints.

My father was a kind, even-tempered man. Up to now he had never beaten me, although he probably had provocation on more than one occasion. This time, however, he stared at me, his face red with anger. He boxed my ears energetically.

These blows again I did not feel, for my surprise was too great. I was more shocked than hurt. My father evidently noticed this at once, since he turned around angrily and ordered me to bed without my supper.

This was the first night I felt alone. In later years I had many such nights. The little word "alone" took on a new meaning for me. Our time has provided frequent opportunity for people to endure this aloneness; still, it's difficult to describe.

Later my father must have learned some details of what had happened, because, some days after, he attempted to set the matter between us to rights, quoting a verse:

"Three times while bullets whizzed,
  We took the mountain by storm."

These lines were from one of the poems we had to learn by heart. It was dedicated to a long-forgotten battle, the assault on Spichern Heights. And it was true: I had been in action three times—not including the draymen.

We were soon on friendly terms again, but such a blow can never be quite forgotten, even if both sides have no greater wish than to do just that. A physical touch creates a new relationship. One has to resign one's self to it.

I have dwelt at length on this experience because it encompassed more than an episode. It repeated itself in my life in the same way that a woman, an enemy, or an accident can return. It recurred, though in a different disguise, with the same cast of characters. When the Asturian affair began, we knew that, although we were used to a good deal of trouble, this time it would be no joke. In the first town we entered, the monasteries had been raided, the coffins in the vaults forced open and the corpses set up in the streets in grotesque groups. Then we knew we had come to a country where no mercy could be expected. We passed a butcher shop in which the corpses of monks hung from meat hooks with a sign *"hoy motado,"* meaning "freshly killed." I saw this with my own eyes.

On that day a great sadness overcame me. I knew with certainty that this was the end of everything we had respected and honored. Words like honor and dignity became ludicrous. Again the word "alone" loomed up out of the night. An outrage has an isolating effect, as though our planet were threatened with extinction. I was feverish and thought of Monteron. What would he have said, entering such landscapes? But Monteron's time was past, and men of his type would not have entered in any case. They would have already fallen before the gate, because—"once and for all there are matters I do not wish to know."

At that time my "Day of Spichern" repeated itself with its personnel unchanged; there was but one difference—the Chief whom I tried to seize by the arm was no longer called Hanebut. Neither was the matter in question a bleeding nose. It had more to do with ears. Those whom I helped (as I had the Cossack) again gave me no thanks. On the contrary. Even Weigand reappeared on the scene; now he conditioned the moral climate in a famous newspaper. Without him no one would have known exactly how things should be managed.

Incidentally, on the school playground once, I asked the first Weigand where he had been when the scuffle started.

He said that he had suddenly remembered he hadn't done his homework yet, adding: "It was nasty the way you all pounced on him." He had cut out for himself exactly the piece which suited his purpose. *Cosi fan tutte;* later, too, that was his favorite motto.

XIX

All this came back to me when, after my unpleasant discovery, I was seized more and more irresistibly by weakness. The nausea which I tried to fight off promised nothing good; I had a foreboding that there would be a repetition of what I had endured when I tried to stop Atje Hanebut. And Zapparoni would not let me off so cheaply. I tried, therefore, to comfort myself as one does a sick child. For instance: "Severed ears are lying about on any highway." Or: "You've certainly seen *other* things before, and these are not your concern at all. You'd better take French leave."

Then I tried to recollect episodes from the *History of the Jewish Wars* by Flavius Josephus, who had always been my favorite historian. In those times events happened quite differently. With what massive conviction, with what certainty of a higher mandate and a correspondingly clear conscience did the partners arrive on the scene! The Romans, the Jews in their various factions, the auxiliary peoples, the mountain garrisons which defended themselves to the last man, to the last woman! No decadent blabber here as there would be a hundred years later in Tertullian. Titus had given harsh orders, yet with a dignity as sublime as if he were the spokesman of destiny. Time and again in history there had been periods when action and conviction of right tallied perfectly with each other, a feeling that was shared by all the belligerents and factions concerned. Perhaps Zapparoni had already returned to such a period. Today one had to be part of the game. The closer one stood to the center of the game, the less significant its victims became. People who were in the game, or only thought to be in it, swept away millions, and the masses cheered them. Compared to them, a dismounted cavalryman who had never lifted his weapon against any but other armed men, cut a disreputable figure. It had to stop. Even mentally one had to climb into the tank.

By the way, I still had the rest of Twinnings' money in my pocket; I should have liked to take Teresa out for dinner tonight. I'd take her to the "Old Sweden" and be nice to her. Lately I had neglected her because of my worries. Now I'd tell her that the job with Zapparoni hadn't come off, but that I had a chance of a better opening. She was always afraid I would accept an offer that was beneath me. She had far too good an opinion of me; it had often made me ashamed. Tomorrow I would go to Twinnings and talk with him about the jobs he had not yet mentioned because he did not think I would take them. I might take charge of a gambling table. I'd certainly get involved in scandals that might turn out badly if one wasn't slippery as an eel. Then, one had to accept tips. Old comrades who couldn't stop doing a little gambling—they had learned how in the Light Cavalry—would at first be surprised to see me, but if they had had a run of good luck, they'd slide toward me a red or even a blue chip. One would have to get used to it. But I would know for whom I did it. And I would enjoy it, and would even take on other work. I would tell Teresa that I had an office job.

XX

All these matters I turned over in my mind, but I found no resting place. The whole ship rocked right up to the top of the mast. Though I strictly avoided looking in that direction, my thoughts kept breaking away toward the water hole. My head was still buried in my hands. The Smoky Gray described wide figures of eight in front of me.

My situation had certainly been planned with a purpose. This was obvious if only because the master of the house still failed to appear. Evidently he was either waiting for some result or postponing it. But what kind of result could possibly make sense? I would never be able to leave the park. Should I get up and return to the terrace? Unfortunately I may have shown my reaction too strongly after I had made my discovery.

If, however, my situation had been arranged and, what is more, intended as a dilemma, much depended on the degree of my ability to see through the planned stage effects; then I could choose a direction for my behavior. I might be able to deny that I had seen the object, but perhaps it would be more profitable to respond to the provocation, as was expected. In any case, my remaining in a reflective mood could do no harm, since it was probably anticipated that I would take the discovery seriously and be alarmed. I had to think hard, review the case again, and use all my wits.

The possibility that I had come upon a nest of evil, as I had thought in my first consternation, I now excluded not only as being improbable but as emphatically out of the question. Such an oversight, such an error in staging, was unimaginable in Zapparoni's domain. Nothing took place here that was not part of the plan, and in spite of all the apparent disorder, one had the impression that even the molecules were controlled. I had sensed this at once on entering the park. Besides, who would leave ears lying around, quite near his house, from sheer forgetfulness?

But if it was a question of the horrible sight having been arranged, it was bound to have something to do with my presence here. It must have been included in the parade of automatons as a calculated caprice. To rouse admiration and terror has at all times been a concern of the great. But there must have been stage directions. And who had provided the stage properties?

One could hardly assume that Zapparoni's plant—where even the impossible was possible—kept a supply of ears on hand. Where such things can happen, although they may be kept as secret as possible, rumors inevitably spread. Everyone knows what no one knows. That notorious Nobody walks around freely.

Of course, many things that were discussed behind the scenes at the good grandfather Zapparoni's—like Caretti's disappearance—were not blazed abroad. But mostly they were ordinary things. This business did not fit into Zapporoni's style. And it was out of all proportion to my circumstances. Who was I to be honored by the cutting off of two or three dozen ears? Even the boldest imagination wouldn't dream of such a thing. And as a joke it was beneath the taste of a sultan of Dahomey. I had seen the interior of Zapparoni's house, had seen his face and his hands. These ears must have been a delusion; I must have been the victim of a vision. The air was sultry; the garden seemed to be bewitched and the swirl of automatons had intoxicated me.

Again I put the field glasses to my eyes and focused them on the water hole. The sun was now in the western sky, and all the red and yellow tints became more spectacular. The superior quality of the glass and the proximity of the object left no possible doubt: they must be ears, human ears.

Were they, however, *genuine* ears? Supposing they were imitations, skillfully contrived frauds? No sooner had this idea flashed through my mind than it seemed very likely. The expenditure was minimal, and the intended effect of a test remained. I had once heard that the Freemasons lay out a corpse of wax, and that the novice, about to be initiated, is brought before it in a dimly lighted room and ordered by the Grand Masters to thrust a knife into the body.

Indeed, it was possible, even probable, that I was faced with some sort of puzzle. In a place where glass bees fly about, why shouldn't wax ears lie around as well? The moment of terror was suddenly followed by the solution, by a feeling of gaiety, almost of relief. This was even a witty touch, although at my expense; perhaps it was meant to indicate that in the future I would have to deal with practical jokers.

I now decided to fall in with the joke and play the fool; I'd pretend not to have seen through the trap. Again I buried my face in my hands, but now in order to conceal my growing amusement. Then I took up the field glasses once more: the objects were infernally well done—I might almost say that they surpassed reality. But I was not going to be taken in. After all, one was used to things like these from Zapparoni.

True, I now saw something that took me aback and again sickened me. A big blue fly descended on one of these shapes, a fly like those one used to see around butcher shops. But, although unpleasant, the sight did not shake my confidence. If I had judged Zapparoni rightly—which I did not in the least pretend to do—this move of his, these ears, could only be artificial. Heads or tails—Zapparoni or King of Dahomey.

We cling to our theories and fit the phenomena to them. The fly? The work of art was to all appearance so perfect that not only my eyes but the insect itself was deceived. It is generally known that birds pecked at the grapes painted by Apelles. And I had once watched a small fly hovering around an artificial violet I wore in my buttonhole.

Moreover, who in the garden would swear on oath that this was natural, that artificial? Had any person, had any pair of lovers in an intimate conversation passed me, I would not have liked to stake my life and declare whether or not they were flesh and blood. Only recently I had admired Romeo and Juliet on the television screen, and had occasion to see for myself that a new and more beautiful era in dramatic art had started with Zapparoni's automatons. How tired one had become of the heavily made-up actors who became more insignificant from decade to decade, and how badly heroic action and classical prose, to say nothing of verse, suited them! In the end, one would no longer have known what a body, what passion, what singing really was, had not Negroes been imported from the Congo. Zapparoni's marionettes were of a quite different proficiency. They needed neither make-up nor beauty contests where chests and hips are measured and compared—they were made to order.

I am not, of course, going to proclaim that they excelled human beings—that would be absurd after all I have said about horses and riders. On the other hand, I think that they set man a new standard. Once upon a time statues and paintings influenced not only fashion but man. I am convinced that Botticelli created a new race and that Greek tragedy enhanced the human body. That Zapparoni attempted something similar with his automatons revealed that he rose far above technique, using media as an artist to create works of art.

For magicians like those Zapparoni employed in his workshops and laboratories, it was a trifle to create a fly. In an inventory which included artificial bees and artificial ears, one must admit the possibility of an artificial fly as well. Therefore, even though loathsome and needlessly realistic—this sight could not disconcert me.

In any case, during this strenuous testing and watching, I had lost the capacity of distinguishing between the natural and the artificial. I became skeptical of individual objects, and, in general, I separated imperfectly what was within and what without, what landscape and what imagination. The layers, close one upon the other, shifted their colors, merged their content, their meaning.

This was pleasant after my previous experiences. And most welcome was the fact that the business of the ears had lost its inner weight. I had been needlessly nervous. Of course they were artificial—or artificially natural—and, as with marionettes, pain becomes meaningless. Because this is indisputable, it even stimulates people to cruel jokes. It does not matter much so long as we know that the doll, whose arm we tear out, is of leather, or that the Negro we use as a target is of papier-mâché. We like to aim at human forms.

But here the world of marionettes became very powerful and developed a subtle, carefully reasoned out play of its own. The marionettes became human and stepped into life. Leaps, drolleries, caprices—which only rarely had been thought of before—now became possible. Defeatism no longer existed. I saw the entrance to a painless world. Whoever passed into it was protected against the ravages of time. He would never be seized by a feeling of awe. Like Titus he would enter the destroyed temple, the burnt-out Holy of Holies. Time held its trophies and its wreaths ready for him.

XXI

Out of this trap could come my chance for a great career at Zapparoni's. I had only to intimate that I was delighted with the spectacle he had staged—that it whetted my appetite. I would take the whole thing as a symbol of sovereignty, as the fasces and axes proper to the Consul Romanus. If I succeeded in overriding my scruples and shaking off my defeatism, I need not walk before Zapparoni as a minor lictor—I could with confidence compete with Fillmor.

However, I had often reached this point before, when my failures made me miserable. In those cases, as here, I would waste my time, in an embarrassing situation, in doing nothing, and then shrink back from some kind of brutality that is nowadays quite inevitable. One could be sure that even here, while developing the ideas of a municipal tyrant, I would not be capable of even touching one of these ears, artificial or not. It was really ridiculous.

What would Zapparoni think if I touched an ear? He had warned me only against the bees. Probably he was looking for exactly that man who *is* capable of touching ears. I took up one of the hand nets, which was leaning against the pavilion, and walked toward the water hole. There I selected one of the ears and fished it out. It was a large, well-shaped, perfectly reproduced ear, the ear of a grown man. I was sorry not to have a magnifying glass with me, but my eyesight was good enough.

I placed my catch on the garden table and touched it confidently with my hand. I must admit that the replica was excellent. The artist had gone so far in his naturalism that he had not even forgotten the tiny tuft of hair, characteristic of the ear of a mature man, which is generally trimmed with a razor blade. He had, moreover, indicated a small scar—a romantic touch. It was clearly evident that Zapparoni's workers did not work for money alone. They were craftsmen of a supernatural precision.

The Smoky Gray had again come close, and only slightly vibrating, it now hovered almost motionless in mid-air, its feelers jutting forth. I did not pay any attention to it, keeping my eyes fixed on my object, which stood out in bold relief against the green table top.

In school we learned that any object we gaze at for a long time, appears again, when we turn our eyes away from it, as a kind of afterimage. We see it on the wall when we stare at it, or on the inner side of our lids when we close them. It frequently limns itself sharply against a background and even reveals details we did not consciously perceive before. Only the color has changed, reflecting the phenomenon on the retina in a new light. Similarly, when I looked at this ear, I felt for a short moment slightly dizzy, since it wavered before my eyes in a delicate green brilliance while the table top stood out in red.

Objects which enthrall us also present a mental afterimage, an intuitive counterimage which reveals that part of perception which we have suppressed. Suppression takes place in any perception; to perceive means to eliminate.

When I had examined the ear, I had done so wishing that it were a hoax, an artifice, a doll's ear, that it had never known pain. But now that it appeared to me as an afterimage, it revealed that from the very beginning—for all the time since I had been looking at it—I had comprehended it as the focal point of this garden, and that the sight of it had formed in my mind the word "hear." When in Asturia they had dragged the corpses out of their tombs in order to abjure humanity, we knew that after such a reception only evil could be in store for us—that we had entered through the gates to the nether world.

In this place, however, a mind was at work to negate the image of a free and intact man. The same mind had devised this insult: it intended to rely on man power in the same way that it had relied on horsepower. It wanted units to be equal and divisible, and for that purpose man had to be destroyed as the horse had already been destroyed. The signals flashed at the entrance gates. Anyone who approved of them, or who only failed to recognize them for what they were, would be unsuitable.

XXII

It was a terrible signal, a ticket for admission. In the same way, procurers who wish to lead us into disreputable places press into our hands an obscene picture. My daemon had warned me.

When I saw through the plot, I was seized with a blind fury.

An old soldier, a Light Cavalryman and pupil of Monteron, waited obsequiously before a shop where cut-off ears were displayed while in the background someone chuckled. Up till now I had always fought with decent weapons, and I had quit the service before the abominable warmongers contrived their murderous incendiaries. But here the new subtleties were prepared in a lilliputian style. As always, the primary concern was with the lowering of "curtains" in order to let the surprises ripen. There'd be no lack of policemen; indeed, countries already existed where everyone shadowed everyone else and, should that not be enough, denounced himself. This was no business for me. I had seen enough; I preferred the gambling casino.

I knocked the table over and kicked the ear out of the way. Now the Smoky Gray became very lively and flew up and down like a scout who wants to enjoy an operation from every perspective. I grabbed the golf bag, pulled out one of the stronger irons, and made a wide sweeping stroke. As I took my stance, I heard a short warning call, like the ones heard in air-raid shelters. But I ignored it and, having turned round on my axis, I hit the Smoky Gray with the flat end of the iron and smashed it. I saw a coil of wire spring out of its belly. Several sparks followed, as if a toy frog were exploding, and from the iron golf club rose a rust-brown cloud. Again I heard a voice: "Close your eyes." A splash hit me, burning a hole in the sleeve of my coat. Another voice called that there was a skin ointment in the pavilion. I found it in a sort of air-raid emergency kit, which I remembered having seen before. My arm showed not a sign of injury; the explosion hadn't left a single suspicious mark.

The calls sounded synthetic, as if they were coming out of a mechanical dictionary. Like traffic signals, they had a sobering effect. I had been acting on impulse without consulting my reason. It was the mistake I always made when provoked. I had to correct it. I promised myself even to swallow insults at the casino, and was confident that I'd be able to do so. First, however, I had to get out of here; the job, of course, now being out of the question.

Moreover, I had completely lost any desire to occupy myself with Zapparoni's private hobbies. Possibly I had seen too many of them already.

XXIII

The sun, now on the decline, was still shining warmly on the paths, and it was again quiet, even peaceful, in the park. Bees, real bees, were still humming about the flowers, while the weird automatons had vanished. Very likely the creatures of glass had been enjoying a field day, a grand review.

The day had been long and hot; slightly dazed, I stood in front of the pavilion and stared down the path. At its turn I saw Zapparoni walking toward me. Why, seeing him, was I seized with fear? I do not mean the kind of terror a dictator spreads at his approach. This was more a vague feeling of guilt, of bad conscience, as I waited for him. In the same way I once stood, dirty faced, in my tattered suit in our hall at home, when my father came in. And why should I try to push the ear under the overturned table with my foot so he'd not see it? I did it less to conceal my curiosity from him than from a feeling that the ear was not a sight fit for him.

Slowly he walked along the path and came up to me. Then he stopped before me and fixed me with his amber-colored eyes. They had now turned to a deep, dark brown, with light inclusions. His silence oppressed me. At last I heard his voice: "But I told you to beware of the bees."

He took the golf club in his hand and examined the corroded metal head. It was still spluttering. He cast a cursory glance at the smoky-gray splinters and then looked at the sleeve of my coat. I had the impression that nothing escaped his notice. He said: "Well, at least you caught one of the harmless ones."

It did not sound unkind. I hadn't the slightest idea of the price of such a robot. But since it had most likely been a model piece, probably it far exceeded the total of all the wages I would have earned if I had been hired. The thing must have been crammed full of apparatuses.

"You've been imprudent. These mechanisms aren't golf balls."

Even this sounded benevolent, as if he didn't overly disapprove of my golf stroke. I could not even contend that the Smoky Gray had an evil design on me. I had lost my nerve, as the saying goes. Its fluttering about, while I examined the ear, had exasperated me. But the ear alone, or rather ears, would have been ample reason for losing your nerve. For most people, after all, a sight like that is not exactly amusing. However, I did not wish to defend myself. It would be best not to let Zapparoni see the ear at all.

Meanwhile he had already discovered it. He touched it lightly with the golf club and then turned it round with the point of his slippers, shaking his head. His face now completely took on the expression of an irritated parrot. His eyes brightened to a clear yellow and the inclusions disappeared.

"Here you have an example of the crowd I'm cursed with —in a madhouse you can at least lock them up."

After I had righted the table and sat down with him, he

told me the story of the ears. Once more the ears had to go through a transformation in my mind. In fact they *were* cut off, though painlessly, and even my presence here had something to do with this mutilation.

I should know, Zapparoni explained, that the extraordinary impression of life-sized marionettes like Romeo and Juliet, which I had admired, rested less on the faithful reproductions of their bodies than on deliberate deviations. In the matter of faces, ears play an almost greater role than eyes, which can be easily surpassed in shape, mobility, and, of course, color. For noble types one tries to reduce the size of the ears, to improve their shape, their color, and their placement, as well as to give them a certain mobility which intensifies facial play. This mobility, while lost among civilized peoples, can be observed still in animals and primitive races. Moreover, both ears should be slightly asymmetric. For an artist, one ear is unlike another. In this respect it was necessary to educate the public. It had to be taught a higher anatomy. This could only be done over an extended period of time. Neither time nor effort could be spared. Decades would hardly be sufficient.

Well, he did not wish to digress. All these details, and others as well, had been, in the case of the marionettes, in the hands of Signor Damico, a Neapolitan by birth, past master in the fashioning of ears.

Such ears are, of course, not simply stitched on or manufactured by the piece, as a wood carver, a sculptor, or a wax molder would do. On the contrary, they must be organically joined to the body by a method that belongs among the secrets of the new-style marionettes.

The difficulty of this work is still further intensified by the fact that many hands are employed on a single figure. This teamwork leads to quarrels and petty jealousies among the artists, who loathe the collective work. So Signor Damico had made an enemy of everyone, and that because of trifles not worth mentioning. In short, he refused to have anything

to do with the others. But since he did not want them to derive any profit from his work, he cut off with a razor blade all
the ears of the marionettes they had collectively manufactured. After that he went off and away, and it was now feared
that he would practice his art elsewhere, for, since the success of the new movies, other countries had started experi-
menting in the construction of marionettes.

What could be done? If you reported him, he would appeal to his copyright. You would make a fool of yourself. It
would be a scoop for the press. And to marionettes of this
type you could not simply attach a severed ear, any more than
you could to real human beings.

When all this had taken place, Zapparoni had again realized
his vexatious dependence. Had Signor Damico returned, he
would have forgiven him. The man was irreplaceable, since
one does not make ears as easily as one makes children. The
incident had further shown that the supervision in his plant
was not all he could wish. This was the reason why he had
turned to Twinnings. And Twinnings had sent for me.

Incidentally, Zapparoni had actually ordered the ears to be
thrown into the water hole for my benefit, and he had watched
me. This was the practical part of my visit to him. As to the
result—I had not passed; I was unsuited for the position he
had in mind; but he did not supply me with any further information about the kind of work he had intended. Caretti, too,
had been unfit; he was now in a lunatic asylum in Sweden. He
could not be discharged. It was at least an advantage that the
doctors took his pronouncements as pure imagination, the
ravings of a man frightened by hallucinations.

I could go home then. I would remember this day. A load
was off my mind, although I thought of Teresa. She would be
sorry.

I was to sit down once more, however. Zapparoni was ready
with another surprise. Although I had looked at everything
from a different angle than the required one, it seemed that he

had found some merit in my statement about the white flags which he had challenged me to give in his library. He thought I had a certain sense of parity, of the balance that is due to the parts of a whole—that probably I had Libra in my horoscope. He also knew that during the years when I had been testing tanks, I had shown a sharp eye for inventions, although my name was in the Service's black books.

In his plant, he said, new inventions were daily announced, improvements suggested, simplifications devised. Even though the workers were difficult to handle and, like the Neapolitan, were frequently querulous, they were highly gifted crafts-men. And one had to put up with their weaknesses, which were the dark side of their excellences. I could certainly im-agine (he said) that with these ambivalent gifts, there was no lack of feasible projects along with the quarrels and feuds so common among artists. Each man considers his solution the best, and everyone claims to have been the first to have had a bright idea. It was impossible to bring all this to court; what was wanting was an internal court of arbitration. For this he needed a man who combined a sharp eye for technical matters with a power of discrimination: a combination rarely found in one person. He might even be slightly old-fashioned in his views.

"Captain Richard, would you accept this offer? Very well. Then I'll make the arrangements. I trust you will not resent an advance?"

In this way, Twinnings would, after all, get his commission, but he'd get it from Zapparoni; Twinnings helped his com-rades gratuitously.

XXIV

I might now conclude my story as in those novels where one presses on to a happy ending.

Other principles hold good here. Today, only the person who no longer believes in a happy ending, only he who has consciously renounced it, is able to live. A happy century does not exist; but there are moments of happiness, and there is freedom in the moment. Even Lorenz, suspended in nothingness, still had a moment of freedom; he could change the world. They say that during such a fall your whole life passes before you once again. This is one of the mysteries of time. The moment is wedded to eternity.

Soon perhaps, I shall describe in detail the consequences which my position as an arbitrator involved, and my experiences within Zapparoni's domain. (Until now I had been only in the outer courts.) Only a person who does not know the force of destiny will assume that my evil star faded out. We do not escape our boundaries or our innermost being. We do not change. It is true we may be transformed, but we always walk within our boundaries, within the marked-off circle.

That surprises would never be wanting at Zapparoni's should be manifest from this report. He was an enigmatic man, a master of masks, who came out of the virgin forest.

When I saw him approaching me in the garden, I had even felt reverence, as if he were preceded by lictors. His footmarks vanished behind him. I sensed the depth on which he rested. Nearly everyone today is a slave to material means. For him it was a game. He had captivated the children: they dreamed of him. Behind the fireworks of propaganda, the eulogies of paid scribes, something else existed. Even as a charlatan he showed greatness. Everyone knows these people from southern countries over whose cradle Jupiter stands in strong aspect. They often change the world.

All the same, I have repaid his kindness. When he tested me and afterwards gave me my position, I felt something like affection growing in me. It is a good thing when someone comes and says: "We are going to play the game—I'll arrange it." We have confidence in him.

There were rooms into which I had never looked before, and there were also great temptations; until finally my evil star triumphed again. Who knows, however, if my evil star might not be my lucky star? Only the end will tell.

But that evening, driving back to the plant in the little underground train, I firmly believed that my bad luck was over. One of the cars which I had admired that morning took me back to the city. Fortunately some shops were still open here and there; I could buy myself a new suit. For Teresa I bought a nice summer dress with red stripes, which reminded me of the one in which I had seen her for the first time. It fitted to perfection—I knew her measurements. She had shared many hours with me, mainly the bitter ones.

We went out for dinner; it was one of the days one never forgets. Quite soon the happenings in Zapparoni's garden began to fade in my memory. There is much that is illusory in techniques. But I never forgot Teresa's words, and her smile when she spoke. Now she was happy about me. This smile was more powerful than all the automatons—it was a ray of reality.

NOONDAY PAPERBACKS
available at your bookstore

(*continued from front flap*)

...dealing so sharply with the problems of the modern technological world. But Juenger's parable of the mechanical bees, whose efficiency is such that the flowers from which they gather honey die, has historical and philosophical ramifications that make it absolutely unique.

Since the death of Thomas Mann, Ernst Juenger and Herman Hesse are considered the two most important authors writing in Germany. Juenger, born in 1895, is most famous in this country for his novel, *On the Marble Cliffs*.

About the translators: Louise Bogan is one of America's finest poets and critics. Elizabeth Mayer is well known both here and abroad for her many distinguished translations.

Jacket design by Nancy Webb

FARRAR, STRAUS AND CUDAHY
19 Union Square West, New York 3, N. Y.

CPSIA information can be obtained
at www.ICGtesting.com
Printed in the USA
LVHW061811160723
752622LV00047B/1023

 9 781013 589287